"I Just Don't Think It Would Be Wise For Us To Get Involved."

"Why?"

Frustrated that Cecile wouldn't drop the subject, Rand heaved a slow breath. "You're a nice woman, Cecile, but I'm just not prepared to take on a family."

Her eyes grew wide. "A family!" she echoed back at him. "Who the heck asked you to take on my family? Of all the unmitigated gall—"

She swung away from him, muttering under her breath, then whipped back, leveling a finger at his nose. "For your information, Dr. Coursey, I'm not looking for a husband. A lover, yes, I'd consider you for that position. But a husband? No, thanks!"

Dear Reader,

Readers ask me what *I* think Silhouette Desire is. To me, Desire love stories are sexy, sassy, emotional and dynamic books about the power of love.

I demand variety, and strive to bring you six unique stories each month. These stories might be quite different, but each promises a wonderful love story with a happy ending.

This month, there's something I know you've all been waiting for: the next installment in Joan Hohl's *Big, Bad Wolfe* series, July's *Man of the Month, Wolfe Watching*. Here, undercover cop Eric Wolfe falls hard for a woman who is under suspicion.... Look for more *Big, Bad Wolfe* stories later in 1994.

As for the rest of July, well, things just keep getting hotter, starting with *Nevada Drifter*, a steamy ranch story from Jackie Merritt. And if you like your Desire books fun and sparkling, don't miss Peggy Moreland's delightful *The Baby Doctor*.

As all you "L.A. Law" fans know, there's nothing like a good courtroom drama (I *love* them myself!), so don't miss Doreen Owens Malek's powerful, gripping love story *Above the Law*. Of course, if you'd rather read about single moms trying to get single guys to love them—*and* their kids— don't miss Leslie Davis Guccione's *Major Distractions*.

To complete July we've found a tender, emotional story from a wonderful writer, Modean Moon. The book is titled *The Giving*, and it's a bit different for Silhouette Desire, so please let me know what you think about this very special love story.

So there you have it: drama, romance, humor and suspense, all rolled into six books in one fabulous line—Silhouette Desire. Don't miss any of them.

All the best,

Lucia Macro
Senior Editor

Please address questions and book requests to:
Silhouette Reader Service
U.S.: 3010 Walden Ave., P.O. Box 1325, Buffalo, NY 14269
Canadian: P.O. Box 609, Fort Erie, Ont. L2A 5X3

PEGGY MORELAND
THE BABY DOCTOR

SILHOUETTE *Desire*®
Published by Silhouette Books
America's Publisher of Contemporary Romance

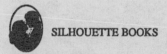

SILHOUETTE BOOKS

ISBN 0-373-05867-5

THE BABY DOCTOR

Books by Peggy Moreland

Silhouette Desire

A Little Bit Country #515
Run for the Roses #598
Miss Prim #682
The Rescuer #765
Seven Year Itch #837
The Baby Doctor #867

PEGGY MORELAND,

a native Texan, has moved nine times in thirteen years of marriage. She has come to look at her husband's transfers as "extended vacations." Each relocation has required a change of careers for Peggy: high school teacher, real-estate broker, accountant, antique-shop owner. Now the couple resides in Oklahoma with their three children, and Peggy is working on a master's degree in creative studies while doing what she loves best—writing!

For my stepfather, Jed Howie,
who accepted three grown daughters and six
grandchildren with the grace, kindness and generosity
for which he is known.
Thanks for all the support and encouragement.
Papa, this one is for you.

One

Though she'd rather have run screaming from the hospital, Cecile clung to her friend Malinda's hand, refusing to let go. "Pant, don't push!" she ordered, her voice stern with a mixture of nerves and fear.

The pain drew Malinda from her back to her elbows. "*You* pant!" she gasped as she tried to wrench her hand away from Cecile. "*I'm* pushing." She gritted her teeth and strained forward, struggling to escape both the pain and Cecile's deathlike grip.

With both hands occupied, fighting to maintain a hold on Malinda, Cecile tucked her nose into the crook of her elbow and wiped at the perspiration beading her forehead and stinging her eyes. She'd given birth three times herself, but didn't remember labor being this intense this quickly. After two hours as Malinda's stand-in Lamaze coach, she wasn't sure how much more she could take. This was her friend suffering, her best friend, and other than Jack, no one loved Malinda more.

Where is that darn Jack Brannan, anyway? He should be here at his wife's side, not me.

Cecile mopped frantically at her friend's damp brow as if that action alone might reduce the pain somewhat. Noting that Malinda's face was contorting and deepening in color, Cecile cried hysterically, "Don't push! Breathe!"

Malinda all but snarled. "I hate you, Cecile."

"Fine," Cecile replied in an equally spiteful tone. "Hate me all you want." She knew as long as Malinda was talking, she was breathing, not pushing, and that was her goal. "But if you want to hate someone, hate Jack. He's the one who got you into this mess."

While she had Malinda's attention diverted, she placed a hand on her friend's swollen abdomen and monitored the progress of the contraction, wondering where in the devil the doctor was. The woman was having a baby, for pity's sake!

The tautness beneath Cecile's hand gradually slackened as the contraction ebbed away. Relieved, Cecile loosened her grip, and Malinda sank back against the pillow, her energy sapped. She stared at the ceiling, her eyes glazed, her chest heaving as if she'd just sprinted a quarter mile race. Somehow she found the strength to laugh, which irritated the hell out of Cecile. "What's so funny?" she snapped impatiently.

"You are," Malinda said, still chuckling as she scraped damp bangs back from her face to better see Cecile. "You're an absolute wreck."

Now that the worst was over for a few minutes, Cecile dropped Malinda's hand and collapsed into the chair beside the hospital bed. "There's gratitude for you," she muttered as she sprawled her feet out in front of her.

"I'm grateful."

"Yeah, right." Cecile thrummed her fingers against the chair arm and narrowed her eyes at the closed door, wondering where the hospital staff had hidden themselves. Weren't they supposed to be hovering around, doing medical miracles or something to insure this baby's safe arrival?

"Don't frown, Cecile. You'll make wrinkles."

The statement was ludicrous considering the situation they were in and sounded so much like Malinda's aunt, Cecile couldn't help but laugh. She dropped her head back on the chair and closed her eyes. "God. You sound just like your Aunt Hattie."

"I could do worse."

"Maybe," Cecile replied lazily, letting memories of Malinda's aunt and her old-maid, spinsterish ways drift through her mind. Agatha Prim's one redeeming quality to Cecile's way of thinking was that she'd taken Malinda in to raise. For that alone, Cecile would be eternally grateful.

Fast friends since the age of twelve when Malinda had moved in with her maiden Aunt Hattie, the two had been inseparable, although opposites. A grin chipped at one corner of Cecile's mouth as she remembered her first glimpse of Malinda. Cecile had been hiding in the branches of the elm tree that separated her parents' home from that of Hattie Prim's. Malinda had walked out her aunt's back door wearing a white dress edged in eyelet lace, white socks and white patent leather shoes. Since Cecile was dressed in her usual summer attire—a pair of her brother's cutoff jeans, a slouchy T-shirt and bare feet—the contrasts between the two girls was telling.

In spite of their differences, the friendship they'd formed that day had lasted twenty years, the last six of which they'd shared partnership in a children's clothing store. Malinda had served as Cecile's maid of honor and godmother to her three children, and now it was Cecile's turn to return the favor. Eighteen months before, she'd served as maid of honor at Malinda's wedding. Today—hopefully—Malinda's first child was to be born and Cecile was to be the baby's godmother.

"Uh-oh."

Instantly alert, Cecile jerked upright, searching Malinda's face for any sign of discomfort. "Another contraction?"

Her lower lip tucked between her teeth, Malinda slowly nodded. A single tear squeezed from eyes squenched tight against the pain.

Cecile was on her feet, grabbing at Malinda's hand. Slender fingers that to the eye appeared barely strong enough to depress a piano key closed over Cecile's and clamped like a vise. Wincing, Cecile stole a glance at the clock. Two minutes apart. Dear God, where is that doctor?

"Breathe, Malinda," she urged, finger-combing her friend's hair from her forehead. "Open your eyes and focus. Don't fight the pain. Work with it."

Another tear coursed down Malinda's cheek, but bravely she opened her eyes and focused on a spot on the ceiling. Gradually her breathing slowed and leveled.

The door behind Cecile quietly opened then closed. She glanced over her shoulder to see a man in green scrubs rounding the end of the bed. He stopped on the opposite side and took Malinda's hand in his. Long, competent fingers moved instinctively to circle her wrist.

"And how's our patient doing?" he asked cheerfully.

Malinda opened her mouth to respond, but only a low, guttural groan came out.

"Breathe, Malinda, breathe!" Cecile ordered, then snapped up her head to glare at the doctor. *And how's our patient doing?* What an asinine question. Couldn't he see the pains were all but ripping her apart?

But the doctor wasn't paying attention to Cecile. His gaze was fixed on the Rolex watch on his wrist. With his head bent, all she could see was the top of his head. A crease—obviously left there by the strings of the mask that now dangled from around his neck—ran from ear to ear, cutting a narrow swath through hair the color of rich, old leather.

Playboy. That was the image he exuded. Razor-cut hair, manicured hands. A glimpse of paler skin exposed beneath the watch when he angled his wrist made her wonder where he'd gotten the tan. Tennis court? Golf course? Isn't that where most doctors spent their free time? Or at least where they told their *wives* they were spending their time?

She watched in silent fury as he finished measuring Malinda's pulse and made a notation on the chart before he finally lifted his eyes to meet hers over Malinda's swollen abdomen. His movements were as slow as a turtle's in Cecile's estimation and his expression a little too relaxed for what the seriousness of the situation dictated, which only pumped up her anger.

She'd spent most of her life protecting Malinda. Of the two, Malinda was the weaker, more delicate one. Cecile had delivered more black eyes than she could count for Malinda's benefit and knew that she'd willingly black this arrogant man's eye, as well, if he didn't do something—and fast—to ease Malinda's pain.

"Are you family?" the doctor asked as he replaced the chart.

"No, but—"

"Then you'll need to step outside while I check her progress."

"But I'm—"

Malinda's fingers clamped down hard on Cecile's, yanking Cecile's attention away from the doctor. She glanced down to see her friend's face twisted in pain. Without thinking, she stretched across the bed, grabbed the front of the doctor's green scrubs and wrenched until his face was within inches of her own.

"Give her something *now!*" she grated through clenched teeth. "Or so help me, I'll—I'll—"

"You'll what?" Though his expression remained impassive, the steely glint in the doctor's eye told Cecile his anger equaled hers.

Her chest swelled and her mind whirled as she tried to think of something low-down and mean enough to threaten him with. "I'll—I'll—"

A tug on her hand had her looking down again.

"Cecile, it's okay," Malinda said, her voice strained but reassuring. "Grab a cup of coffee or something. I'll be fine."

Not wanting to leave her friend alone, but not wanting to upset her further, Cecile wavered uncertainly. "Are you sure?"

"Yes, I'm sure."

Reluctantly, Cecile released Malinda's hand, then more slowly, her grip on the doctor's scrubs. She smoothed damp palms down the sides of her skirt, fighting for calm. "I'll be right outside the door," she said to Malinda as she watched her friend's eyes drift closed. At Malinda's slow nod, she turned her gaze full on the doctor. "But you just holler if you need me. I'll be back in here faster than you can say spit!" The words directed at the doctor were for Malinda's benefit, but the silent warning behind them was all for the man in green.

He acknowledged the threat by arching one eyebrow and looking down his nose at her in a way she knew was meant to intimidate. God, how she hated doctors! With one last, scathing look at him, she wheeled and managed to make it

to the door and out into the hallway before her knees buck-
led. She sagged against the wall. Her heart beat ninety to
nothing and her hands shook so hard she couldn't hold a
cup of coffee even if she'd wanted to.

Malinda was right. She was a wreck. She couldn't stand
to see her friend in so much pain. If she could have the baby
for her, she'd gladly do so, just to have the business over
with.

She took a deep breath and willed her heart to slow down,
but the antiseptic smell unique to hospitals made her stomach knot convulsively. She hated hospitals. The clawing
odor, the bustle of doctors, nurses and orderlies intent on
their work, their guarded whispers suggesting secrets only
they were privy to, secrets in the past that had included her.
Nothing short of her love for Malinda could keep her in this
place.

"Cecile!"

She jumped at the sound of Jack's voice. She spotted him
at the end of the hall by the elevators and took off at a run.
When they met, she threw herself into his arms. "Thank
God, you're here," she said in relief.

"Is something wrong?" he asked, pushing her to arm's
length so he could see her face.

"No. Everything's fine," she assured him. "I was just
afraid you weren't going to make it in time."

"I got here as fast as I could. Where is she?"

Cecile was already tugging him down the hall. "Room
215. The doctor's examining her right now. He made me
leave because I'm not family." She stopped outside the door
but caught Jack's arm before he could slip inside. "He
won't let me in, but you tell that arrogant SOB to give her
something for the pain."

A puzzled frown creased Jack's forehead. "But Malinda
and I decided to have the baby naturally."

She jerked her hand from his arm. "Fine," she snapped. "Then you watch her suffer. I can't." Tears welled and she spun, folding her arms at her breasts and turning her back on him.

A hand came from behind to tentatively light on her shoulder. She tensed beneath it.

"Don't worry, Cecile," he said softly. "I'll take care of her."

She dipped her head, biting at her lower lip to keep the tears that threatened at bay. Jack loved Malinda. He'd proven that to Cecile repeatedly over the past two years. As Malinda's husband, it was his place to care for her, not Cecile's. Remembering this, she lifted a hand to cover his. "I know, Jack. I know. Just get in there. She needs you."

His hand slipped from beneath hers, and she heard the door open behind her. A nurse appeared, her hands filled with a tray of medical paraphernalia. The woman glanced at Cecile, then away, then quickly back again. Cecile saw the spark of recognition and the look of pity that followed.

She should've been accustomed to the looks after spending seven years as Dr. J. Denton Kingsley's wife, and three more as his widow. Most people who had known him pitied her, but none more than the hospital staff who had worked with him. The nurse standing in front of her was a little too old for Denton's taste, but Cecile could tell by the look in her eye that the woman was more than aware of his tomcatting ways.

Lifting her chin a notch, Cecile stared right back. Flustered, the nurse brushed past her to follow Jack into the room. Before the door settled back into place, a low moan drifted out into the hall.

Clapping her hands over her ears, Cecile sank back against the wall.

Oh, why did Eve make Adam eat that apple? she cried inwardly. Just because of that one measly mistake in the Garden of Eden, are women doomed to suffer from now until eternity? All a man has to do is court and woo, deposit his seed and nine months later sit around smoking cigars while the woman suffers all the pain. Where is the justice in it all?

The door whispered open beside her, and Cecile dropped her hands and straightened expectantly. The doctor stepped out and paused as the door closed behind him.

"How is she?" Cecile asked anxiously.

"Fully dilated. We're taking her to delivery."

Cecile reached for the door, but he caught her hand before she could push it open. "You can't go in. The nurse is prepping Malinda, and Jack's changing into his scrubs so he can go into the delivery room with her."

Cecile's face fell and her hand dropped to her side. "Oh."

His expression softened somewhat. "Why don't you go on to the waiting room? It shouldn't be long now."

Her breath came out on a ragged sigh. "All right."

"Do you know where it is?"

"No, but I'll find it."

"I'll show you."

Nervously, Cecile glanced back at the door. "But shouldn't you—"

He slipped his arm through hers, gently guiding her away from Malinda's room. "I promise you, everything's under control. Besides," he added, chuckling, "Jack's an old pro at this. If the baby should decide to arrive before I get there, he could probably deliver it himself."

Jack deliver the baby! Cecile planted her feet, jerking the man to a stop at her side. Her eyes wide, she stared at him in openmouthed disbelief.

Laughing, he patted her hand as he urged her on down the hall. "I was just kidding. I promise you, I'll be there with my catcher's mitt on."

Catcher's mitt! Further incensed, Cecile jerked free of his grasp. This was not the time or place for jokes! For God's sake! Her first godchild was about to be born.

She walked stiffly beside him, her eyes focused directly in front of her. As far as she was concerned, this man lived up to her every expectation of a doctor—rude, arrogant and a little too friendly with members of the opposite sex.

At the door to the waiting room he stopped. She offered him a tight smile as she sailed right past him. "Thanks for the escort, Doc. Oh, and by the way," she added, turning back to face him. "Your catch better be good," she warned in a low, level voice. "Otherwise, you'll have *me* to deal with."

With that she spun on her heel and left him standing in the doorway, his chin tucked to his neck and his brows nearly meeting over his nose.

"Do we get a discount?"

Rand chuckled as he peeled off a surgical glove and moved to slap Jack on the back. "Always looking for a deal, aren't you, Brannan?" He shook his head. "Sorry, buddy, friendship or no friendship, this one's going to cost you double."

He peered over Jack's shoulder at the two red-faced babies nestled in Malinda's arms. *Twins.* After nine years as an obstetrician, it still surprised him when two popped out when he was expecting only one. A sonogram would probably have revealed that she carried two babies, but there had never been a need or concern to order one. He chuckled, thinking Malinda wouldn't have allowed a sonogram, anyway. She'd been hell-bent on doing everything the natural way, which was fine with him, as long as the mother or the baby's health wasn't at risk.

He reached down to touch the miniature hand of the infant closest to him. The baby's fingers curled to make a fist around his. So tiny, so soft, so perfect. He swallowed hard at the wad of emotion that rose in his throat. Though he witnessed birth almost daily, the miracle never ceased to move him. This was what made the long years of schooling and the grueling schedule he maintained all worthwhile.

Shaking his head at his own sensitivity, he withdrew his hand. His job here was complete.

Malinda glanced up at her husband, her face creased with concern. "Oh, Jack. What about Cecile? She's probably worried herself into a frenzy by now."

Rand saw Jack's frown and subsequent hesitation and had spent enough time in the delivery room to understand it. New fathers rarely wanted to leave their wives or their babies and even though Jack had experienced birth four times before with his first wife, Rand knew this situation was just as special for him as the first. He cupped a hand on his friend's shoulder and squeezed reassuringly. "I'll tell her the news. Why don't you stay here and visit with the newest members of the Brannan clan?"

Malinda smiled her relief. "Thanks, Rand." She laughed and looked down at her babies. "Better be prepared to catch her, though. I'm sure Cecile will faint when you tell her we've had twins."

Catch her? Rand couldn't help chuckling as he left the delivery room and headed down the hall toward the waiting room. Malinda's particular choice of words reminded him of Cecile's anger when he'd mentioned to her earlier about having his catcher's mitt ready—an old joke around the obstetrics wing, but one that failed to draw a smile from Malinda's friend.

And since the woman's attitude toward him hadn't been the friendliest, he could only assume she'd rather hit the floor and suffer a concussion than be caught by him . . . and he might just enjoy watching her fall.

A good ten feet from the door to the waiting room, he heard Cecile's voice, pitched high in anger. Frowning, he paused just short of the doorway and listened.

"I don't know anything!" she was saying irritably. "I've been pacing this stupid waiting room for over an hour with not one word on her progress." Her comment was met with silence. Rand peeked around the door to see who she was talking to. He saw her sitting on a chair, her back to him, a phone clutched in one hand while she twisted a lock of hair into a taut rope with the other. The tip of one shoe flicked into sight and out again as she nervously pumped a crossed leg. The room was empty but for her.

"Personally, I think the doctor's an imbecile, and why on earth Malinda chose him as her OB is beyond me."

Again there was a lapse while she listened. *An imbecile, huh?* Pursing his lips, Rand leaned one shoulder against the doorjamb and settled back to eavesdrop. When he'd seen Cecile earlier, his mind had been on his patient, but with Malinda settled comfortably in the recovery room and her babies in the nursery, he allowed his male instincts to take over.

The woman in front of him was a ball of nervous energy harnessed in a very seductive package. He watched the nervous pumping of her foot and craned his neck to follow the tanned curve of leg to the hem of the skirt, which stopped just short of her knee. His interest carried his gaze higher to the swell of breasts beneath a V-necked silk blouse and higher still to the agitated yet graceful movement of her fingers through her hair. Though he'd bet his next weekend off that the aura was unintended, Malinda's friend exuded sexuality.

"I don't care if he did deliver Jack's other kids!" she said, smacking the swinging foot to the floor and coming to her feet. "The man's an arrogant, irresponsible moron, and furthermore—" she caught the phone cord in her hand and spun around, twisting the cord into a tight knot in her fist "—he—" Her gaze met Rand's and the rest of the statement died on her lips. Her face went as white as the wall behind her. The receiver slipped from her fingers and hit the carpet with a thump. "What's happened?" she whispered weakly.

Remembering Malinda's warning, Rand pushed away from the wall and crossed the room. He picked up the receiver from the floor, then caught Cecile by the elbow and guided her back to the chair. She sank onto it, her gaze riveted on his face. A female voice, distant but distinct, called from the receiver, "Cecile! Cecile! What's going on?"

At the sound of alarm in the voice, Rand lifted the receiver to his ear. "This is Dr. Coursey. May I help you?" He smiled when he recognized the voice of Jack's secretary. He dropped into the seat next to Cecile. "Well, hello, Liz. Long time no see."

He glanced at Cecile as he listened to Liz's reply. "No, everything's fine," he assured her. "Mother and babies are resting well." At the plurality of the word baby, Cecile's eyes bugged wide and her face went whiter than white. Assuming she was about to faint, Rand calmly placed the palm of his hand against the back of her neck and pushed until her face rested between her knees. "Yes," he said into the receiver. "You heard me right. Twins."

"Twins?" Cecile repeated, her words muffled by her knees. "Did you say *twins?*" When he didn't respond, she squirmed beneath the weight of his hand, but he simply increased the pressure to hold her in place.

To Liz's question, he replied, "Girls. The boys should be happy about that. They wanted a sister, and now they've got two." He chuckled again. "Yes, Liz, I'll give them your love. Oh, wait a minute," he added before she could hang up. "Better buy your boss some cigars with pink wrappers instead of blue. I think Jack was expecting another boy." Laughing, he stretched across Cecile's back to replace the receiver but was careful not to loosen his hold on her. She was a little thing, but stronger than an ox and madder than a wet hen. He feared what she'd do if he released her.

He bent until his face was level with hers. Eyes as startling a blue as any newborn baby's met his. He let his gaze drift down a pert nose, noting the flush of temper on her cheeks and full lips set in an angry slash. Shoulder-length hair draped one shoulder and beneath it tendons stood out on her neck.

She didn't look to Rand like some weak-kneed Southern belle who'd swoon at the drop of a hat. She looked more like a mud wrestler and was sure as hell as strong as one, judging by the amount of muscle it was taking to keep her in place. "Are you feeling better now?"

"I would be if you'd let me up," she grated through clenched teeth. She shot him a look that would kill, but Rand simply smiled at her.

A sixth sense told him he better not let her go just yet. That temper of hers had him worried a bit. He'd gotten a taste of it in the labor room when she'd grabbed him by the front of his scrubs and again when she'd laid the threat on him that if things didn't go to her way of thinking in the delivery room, he'd have her to deal with.

Remembering this, he bit back a grin. "Malinda wanted me to tell you she had twins."

Cecile sucked in a frustrated breath. "I heard. Now will you please let me up?"

"She also said you might faint. Are you prone to fainting?"

"No, but I might if you don't let me up so I can breathe."

He dodged an elbow jabbed in his direction and decided for safety's sake—his own—he better do as she asked. He straightened and slowly released his grip on her.

Once free, she snapped back against the chair like a slingshot stretched taut then released. She inhaled deeply, filling her lungs with a cleansing breath, then slowly blew the air out through her teeth. She twisted in the chair to face him, her eyes snapping. "Are you crazy, or what?"

He wrinkled his brow and looked at her askance. "No. Why do you ask?"

She leapt to her feet. "Because you act crazy." She paced across the room, needing to distance herself from the doctor. With the width of the room between them, she turned and leaned against the wall, her arms folded at her chest. A good thirty seconds of silence hummed between them before she asked in a tight voice, "Malinda's okay?"

He mimicked her posture and won a frown. "Yes, she's fine."

"And the babies?"

"Small, but healthy."

She took another deep breath and glanced down at her feet, unable or unwilling to meet his gaze any longer. He stared at the top of her honey blond head and tried his darnedest to remember if he'd ever met her before. Considering she was Malinda's friend and he Jack's, it was surprising their paths hadn't crossed, especially since Malinda had tried fixing him up with every available female within a sixty-mile radius of Edmond, Oklahoma.

But maybe she wasn't available. That thought drew a frown. He looked for a ring, but her left hand was hidden from view.

"Do you hate all men, or is it just me?" he asked.

Her head snapped up at the question, a frown thinning lips a moment before had looked full and darn kissable. "I don't hate men."

"Could have fooled me."

Cecile forced her arms to her sides and stepped away from the wall ashamed of her behavior and her weakness. "I just don't like doctors." She glanced around the room and suppressed a shudder. White walls, soothing music, subdued lighting. Everything to make the visitor feel comfortable and relaxed. Crossing her arms to rub at the goose bumps, she added, "Or hospitals, either, for that matter."

"How long have you had this adversity?"

Her hands stilled and she met his gaze again, one brow raised appraisingly. "Are you an obstetrician or a psychiatrist?"

"I had training in both."

She rolled her eyes. "I should have known."

"Why?"

"All doctors are know-it-alls."

"And you've had enough experience with doctors to substantiate this claim?"

"A lifetime's worth."

He wrinkled a brow in question.

"My ex was a surgeon." She lifted her hand, then let it drop as if that explained everything. For Rand, it didn't, but for the moment he decided to let the statement ride.

"Ex," he repeated thoughtfully. "Divorced?"

"Widowed." She shoved her hands deep into the pockets of her blazer... and, so it seemed, the conversation topic along with them. "So," she said, pasting on a smile too bright to be sincere. "When can I see Malinda and my god-daughters?"

Rand continued to stare at her for a moment, his thoughts focused on what she'd said and the glimpse of pain she'd hidden behind the smile. He couldn't help wondering who her ex was and what he'd done for her to have such a low opinion of doctors and the medical community in general.

Rand was a fixer. He'd spent most of his youth and the better part of adulthood "fixing" other people's problems. And even though he knew this about himself and knew even more that this woman hadn't asked for his help, he couldn't stop that old tug pulling at him, saying *make it better.*

But the artful change of subject and the overbright smile she'd turned on him told him she wasn't in the mood to an- swer any more questions at the moment, not the ones he wanted and needed answered to get to the bottom of her problem.

Time was what he needed. Hoping to buy some more of it with her, he glanced at his watch. "Another fifteen min- utes or so and she should be in her room. The babies should be in the nursery by now, though. Would you like to take a peek at them while you wait?"

Her eyes brightened. "Could I?"

"Sure." He offered his arm. "If the nurses give us any static, I'll just pull rank on them."

He watched her eyes go from shiny bright to tempered steel in a matter of seconds. Pointedly ignoring his offered arm, she turned, her nose aimed at the ceiling. "No special favors for me, thank you. I'll look at the babies through the window like any other visitor."

Rand stared at the back of her head as she walked away, more confused than he'd ever been in his life. The woman's moods changed faster than those of a postpartum mother.

Sighing, he followed her, determined that she wasn't leaving the hospital until he found out why she hated doctors . . . or at the least, her telephone number.

Two

Rand didn't get either of the answers he wanted. Not a reason for Cecile's adversity to doctors and sure as hell not her telephone number. Part of the problem was due to the fact that another of his patients had gone into labor and he'd been paged to the delivery room. The biggest part of the problem was that Cecile wouldn't give him the time of day, and that bugged him. He couldn't figure out what he'd done to deserve her animosity.

On the wild chance she might still be at the hospital, after settling in his last patient, Rand detoured by the nursery. A quick scan of the hallway and the nursery beyond proved she wasn't there. Frustrated and more than a little weary from the long day he'd put in, he leaned his forearm against the cool glass partition and his forehead in the crook of his elbow and stared at the babies.

Visits here always gave him a sense of peace, a sense of rightness about his particular avocation. A smile quirked one side of his mouth as he watched a baby's tiny fist beat the air before finding its way to its mouth. It took so little to pacify an infant. A dry bottom, a warm breast to suckle, the security found in being snuggled close. As he looked at the babies, he wondered which, if any, were lucky enough to be born to parents who'd be willing to fulfill all those needs.

Two for sure would, he reflected as he checked identification cards posted on each bassinet, looking for the name Brannan. Malinda and Jack would see to it that the twins never lacked for anything.

A frown puckered his brow when he read the last card and hadn't found their names. Like Cecile, the babies were nowhere in sight. He hadn't a clue where Cecile might be, but he suspected where he might find the twins. Knowing Malinda, he was sure she'd insisted on having them in her room so she could care for them herself.

Envy pricked at his chest as he thought of his friend's wife. Jack was one lucky guy. Malinda was a beautiful woman, soft-spoken, feminine, loving, kind. Just the kind of woman he'd like for himself, but quite a contrast to her friend Cecile.

Cecile. His thoughts went full circle, back to the woman who'd drawn him to the nursery in the first place and the questions she'd raised in his mind. Still wanting answers, but suspecting he'd never hear them from Cecile, he headed for Room 215.

He stuck his head around the door. "And how's my favorite new mother today?"

Malinda turned a tired but radiant smile on him and waved him in. "Wonderful! Absolutely wonderful."

Just as he'd suspected, two bassinets were parked beside her bed. He bent over the one closest to him and tweaked the baby under the chin. "And the girls?"

"Angels." She let out a contented sigh as she leaned across the bed and propped her cheek on her palm to admire them with him. "Aren't they the most beautiful babies in the world?"

Rand chuckled as he nipped the blanket in closer to the infant's chin. "Without a doubt."

Satisfied with his reply, she eased back against her pillow and adjusted the covers modestly over her raised knees. "So tell me, Dr. Coursey, what are you doing here? Rounds were over hours ago, weren't they?"

Though he loved Malinda dearly, Rand didn't dare just come right out and tell her he'd dropped by to quiz her about Cecile. Malinda might mistake his questions for more than curiosity, and he didn't need that particular complication. In need of an excuse to remain in the room to pick her brain, Rand pulled the chart from its rack and began to flip pages, pretending interest. "Yes, but I thought I better check on you before I headed home."

"Well, I'm fine. Not that I don't appreciate the extra attention, but I'm sure you have better things to do than hover around here."

"Nothing pressing."

"There should be."

He arched a brow her way. "Don't you ever give up?"

Malinda smiled sweetly. "Never. At least not until you've found someone to make your life complete."

He flipped another page. "My life *is* complete."

"You know very well what I mean."

The problem was, he did know. Lately the same concern had nagged at him, making it harder and less enjoyable to go home to an empty house each day.

"Want to dump Jack and make my life complete?" he teased.

"I'd be flattered if I thought you were serious . . . but not tempted."

Chuckling, Rand ran a thumbnail under the last page. "The story of my life. Jack coming by?" he asked off-handedly as he closed the metal binder and replaced the chart.

"Soon, I hope. They had a ball game tonight, but he promised to visit as soon as he put the boys to bed." She smiled. "He said he wanted to tuck his girls in, too."

Four boys by Jack's first wife and now two girls by his second. Six kids total. The mere thought of it made Rand's head spin. He couldn't imagine eight people under one roof—no, the problem was he *could* imagine it. When he and Jack had lived together in the Baxter's foster home, nine kids and two adults had called the place home. Sleeping three to a room hadn't bothered Jack in the least. In fact, he'd seemed happier than a dog with a new bone. Rand was the one who had suffered.

But this is Jack's to deal with, not mine, he reminded himself. Knowing this, he said, "I know he'll be glad to get you all home."

"He will at that." Malinda narrowed an eye at Rand as she watched him tip up the edge of a florist's card. "Is there something on your mind?"

Rand's head snapped up. "No. Why?"

She shrugged a slim shoulder. "I don't know. You just seem edgy."

He shrugged as he dropped the card. "No, just nosy." Still stalling, he strode to the bedside table and thumbed up the lid on the pitcher to check the water level. He was going to have to get to the point pretty quick. He was running out of excuses to stay. "I gave your friend Cecile the news about the twins. Did she come by?"

"No." Malinda smiled as she smoothed the wrinkles out of her bed covers. "But I'm not surprised. For her to have stayed as long as she did is a miracle."

With the topic now open, Rand dropped a hip onto the foot of the bed. "Why?"

"Cecile hates hospitals. Especially this one."

"Bad experience?"

"You could say so."

Her reply was vague enough to keep Rand from pushing—but not enough to make him drop the subject entirely. "Considering she's such a good friend of yours, I'm surprised our paths haven't crossed."

Malinda's lips formed a thoughtful pucker. "Not surprising really. Jack and I discussed introducing the two of you, but considering how Cecile feels about doctors..." Malinda let the statement sort of drift off.

Rand decided it was time to push. "And how is that?"

"She hates them."

All the muscles in Rand's neck slowly unwound. "Thank goodness," he said in relief before he thought better of it.

"What?"

"She said as much, but I was afraid it was just me."

Malinda laughed. "Why? Was she rude?"

"Not rude exactly. More like..." He thought for a moment, then chuckled as he remembered Cecile's description of him to Jack's secretary. "Yeah, rude probably says it best."

"I'm sorry, Rand," she said as she leaned over to console him with a pat on his hand. "She really is a nice person. She just has this thing about doctors."

"She mentioned her husband was a surgeon."

Malinda's eyes narrowed at the mention and she settled back against her pillows. "Yes, he was. Dr. J. Denton Kingsley."

Rand knew the name. And more, the reputation behind it. "Oh..." He frowned, then cocked his head to look at Malinda. "I think I understand why she—"

The door swung wide, capturing both Malinda's and Rand's attention. A bouquet of balloons appeared, about two dozen all in pink, with curls of pink and white ribbon corkscrewing in every direction. Beneath the bouquet, a pair of well-formed tanned legs, dirty white socks and scuffed Reebok tennis shoes protruded.

A feminine voice cried out from the midst of color. "Help me, Jack, or they're all going to pop!"

The top of Jack's head bobbed behind the bouquet. Balloons rubbed together, making that awful screeching noise reminiscent of fingernails on blackboards as Jack worked to punch and shove the mass of balloons through the doorway. Rand jumped up and ran to hold the door wide. Malinda simply watched, her hands smothering her laughter.

"Ouch! That was me!" came Cecile's indignant voice.

"Sorry," Jack replied. "Looked like a balloon to me."

"Very funny, Brannan."

The bouquet touched the ceiling, exposing a rosy-cheeked, breathless Cecile and a grinning Jack. Fresh from the Little League baseball game where they shared coaching responsibilities of their sons' team, both wore black shorts and matching T-shirts with White Sox emblazoned across the front. Jack shrugged, while a smile bloomed on Cecile's face.

"Congratulations, Mom!" Cecile let the strings loose, and the balloons shot to the ceiling as she darted under them, heading for the bassinets. "Oo-oh, aren't they darling?" she cooed as she thumbed a ball cap to the back of her head, then braced her hands on her knees. She leaned in for a closer look before lifting her gaze to Malinda. "Can I pick one up?"

"Sure."

Carefully, Cecile wiped her hands down her thighs, then gently gathered a baby into her arms. Cuddling the infant to her cheek, she strolled to the window. "Hi there, precious. I'm your Aunt Cecile. Want to see the man in the moon?"

If she'd said she *was* the man in the moon, she couldn't have surprised Rand more. He watched her nuzzle the baby, first cheek-to-cheek, then nose-to-nose. The contrasts were shocking. Baseball uniform, dirty tennis shoes and a voice as soft and mellow as warm whiskey. She handled the baby without the egg-in-hand fear most people displayed with newborns—yet another contrast to the tomboy image she projected.

Jack dropped a brown paper bag on the foot of the bed, then jumped to snag the ends of the balloon strings. He glanced back at Rand as he tied them to the foot of the bed. "Better close the door before the nurses think we're having a party in here and kick us all out."

"Yeah, right," Rand said absently, but let his grip on the door relax.

Cecile spun at the sound of his voice, her eyes turning as hard as glass when she spied him. After staring a moment, she flicked her gaze to Malinda's, finding a smile as she dismissed Rand without so much as a hello. "Who am I holding?"

"Madison."

Cecile moved to peer into the other bassinet. "And who is this young lady?"

"Lila."

"Madison and Lila. I like that." She laid down one baby only to pick up the other. "Hello, darling," she said as she lifted the baby for inspection. "Boy, are we going to have fun," she whispered conspiratorially as she headed back to the window. "Your Aunt Cecile's going to teach you to play baseball and tennis and water ski and…" The remainder of her promises were lost to Rand as her voice was drowned by Malinda's.

"Where are all the children?"

"Cecile's parents took them out for pizza."

"Who won the game?"

"We did! Jack, Jr., pitched a no-hitter."

Malinda's smile couldn't have been any prouder if Jack, Jr., had been her own son and not a stepson. "That's my boy! Did he pitch the whole game?"

"No, just three innings. Cecile made me put in Joey."

"And good thing she did. We don't want to wear out Jack, Jr.'s, arm."

Madison fussed, and Jack stepped over to the bassinet. "Hey, sweetheart." He scooped her up, cradling her head in the palm of his hand and her body down the length of his arm. "You feeling ignored?" He held her out in front of him and his smile broadened when she quieted and blinked up at him. "She looks like you," he said as he turned a loving gaze on Malinda.

She tried not to look pleased, but failed miserably. "Maybe a little, but she has your nose."

Watching and listening, Rand choked on a laugh. *Jack's nose?* God, he hoped not. But maybe Madison's would be prettier than Jack's if she stayed out of fights and didn't get it broken as many times as her dad.

Although being in the room with all of them was a hell of a sight more entertaining than going home, Rand couldn't help but feel he was intruding on family time. "Guess I'll be going. Have the nurses page me if you need anything, Malinda."

"Whoa, not so fast." Jack shifted Madison to Malinda's arms and reached for the bag he'd set on the foot of the bed.

He pulled out a bottle and plastic champagne glasses. "We were going to make a little toast."

Rand frowned and glanced at the closed door, suspecting that any second one of the Sisters of Mercy would barge in and rap their knuckles for breaking hospital rules.

Jack chuckled. "Don't worry, Rand. It's alcohol free. See?" He held up the bottle for inspection.

Rand heaved a sigh of relief and damned his own gullibility. Jack had always had a knack for duping him, one that had first surfaced in the foster home they'd shared until Rand had gone away to college, and one that had persisted throughout the years of their friendship.

While Rand strove to recover his composure, Jack popped the cork. Alcohol-free champagne bubbled into plastic. With a receiving blanket draped over his arm, Jack passed the glasses around. Rand accepted his still fighting the feeling of the Goody Two Shoes, easy-to-fool image he'd grown up with.

Once everyone had a flute of champagne, Jack motioned both Cecile and Rand to gather around Malinda's bed. Cecile obeyed, but cut a wide berth around Rand as she juggled Lila in the crook of her arm and the champagne glass in her free hand.

With Rand on one side of him and Cecile on the other, Jack raised his glass in a toast. "To new life and old friends. Thank you both for the part you played in getting these babies here safely."

Plastic clicked as four hands met over the center of the bed to tap glasses. Jack took a sip, then gestured toward Rand with his glass. "I don't know if you know this or not, Cecile, but Rand here delivered my boys, too. Heck of a good doctor and a good friend, as well."

Embarrassed by the praise, Rand shifted his gaze, only to find Cecile staring at him. She frowned and looked away.

Jack cleared his throat, biting back a grin as he glanced down at his wife. "Since they're both here, I think this is as good a time as any, don't you, honey?"

She smiled, her eyes filled with a love for her husband that made Rand feel a stab of envy. "Perfect."

All teasing disappeared from his expression as Jack turned to Rand. "When the boys were born, I never thought much about godparents or guardianship if something were to happen to me and the boys' mother. Then Laurel died and, well...it made me think about the future and the kids' future. Then I met Malinda." He turned a loving gaze on his wife before looking to Cecile. "As you know, Malinda and I want you to be the godmother of the girls.

"And Rand," he said, turning to his friend and draping an arm around his shoulder to pull him closer within the circle. "You're the closest I've ever come to having a brother and probably the best friend I've ever had. Malinda and I have discussed this at great length and hope that you'll be willing to be the girls' godfather and share in the responsibility of their care along with Cecile should something ever happen to Malinda and I."

Rand swallowed hard, at once proud and overwhelmed to have this distinction placed on him. "I'd—"

Jack held up a hand, interrupting Rand. "Before you give me your answer, you better know the rest." He moved to sit on the bed beside Malinda and gathered her hand in his. "We'd also like for the two of you to be guardians of the boys."

Knowing how Jack felt about his kids, Rand knew the amount of trust involved in this request. He also knew the responsibilities he'd be undertaking in the event something happened to Jack and Malinda. But Rand was never one to run from responsibility, no matter how great the weight.

"I'd be honored."

As every eye turned expectantly toward her, Cecile felt her stomach knot convulsively. This wasn't what she'd agreed to when Malinda had asked her to be godmother! And it wasn't the fact that they were throwing in guardianship of the boys that concerned her. She was raising three children on her own, thank you very much, and adding two more—or six more, for that matter—didn't concern her one whit. Besides, she loved Jack's kids like her own.

But a godfather? Someone she'd have to discuss things with, compromise with and share responsibilities with? She cut a glance to Rand and added another twist to her features . . . this time around the mouth. Nobody had said anything about a godfather being in the picture.

Concerned by her friend's continued silence, Malinda prodded, "Cecile?"

Cecile snapped her head around to Malinda. The questioning look on her friend's face had her shifting uncomfortably from one foot to the other. "Well . . ." she began hesitantly. Helplessly, she glanced from Malinda to Jack. His eyes mirrored the same look of puzzlement she'd seen in Malinda's. Feeling trapped, she scrunched up her nose and glanced again at Rand.

The eyes that met hers were intelligent, intense and bed-room soft. This time she found she couldn't look away. She tried to name the emotion she found in his eyes that held her. Surprise? Yes, he was as surprised by her hesitancy as Malinda and Jack, but that wasn't it. Pity? No. It wasn't pity. Cecile Kingsley would never be attracted by pity. Understanding? Yes, maybe a little, but that wasn't what held her captive.

Attraction. Pooh, she thought with a mental snort. If it was, it was one-sided. Playboys, especially those who wore the title doctor, didn't do a thing for Cecile. She frowned as she continued to stare at him. Then it hit her. Compassion.

Oh, God, yes, she thought, her knees going soft. That was it. Compassion was what warmed those brown soulful eyes and drew her in. The kind of compassion that curled up around you like a lover, twining its arms around you and making you feel safe and loved and understood.

He looked at her as if he could read her soul and knew her innermost thoughts, and in knowing, he offered both love and understanding. The urge to slip to his side, to let the warmth of that compassion envelope her was overpowering. She steeled herself against the pull. She didn't need a man's compassion any more than she needed a man's love. Years had gone into the convincing of that, but she'd finally proved it to herself and wouldn't fall into that trap again.

"You haven't changed your mind, have you?" Malinda asked in concern.

Horrified that Malinda would think such a thing, Cecile cried out, "No!" The explosive sound was like a gunshot in the room. Startled by the unexpected noise, the baby in her arms cried, and Cecile soothed. A wistful smile trembled at her lips as she looked down into the face of the infant in her arms. "No," she repeated more softly. "I want to be their godmother."

But god*parent?* She stole another glance at Rand. Sharing the responsibility of raising children with a man she didn't even know? And a doctor, at that. A shiver chased down her spine.

She closed her eyes, blocking out his image. Calm down, she told herself. The chances of Malinda and Jack dying simultaneously and leaving the kids in our care are bound to be one in a million. But the odds had never been in Cecile's favor. Not in keeping a man at home and not in preventing her from becoming a widow at the age of twenty-nine.

But she wouldn't let Malinda down. Not now, and not ever. Even if it meant sharing godparent responsibilities with Dr. Rand Coursey. She opened her eyes and turned them full on Malinda. "I'd be honored to be *all* your children's godmother. But," she added sternly, "you have to promise me one thing."

"What?"

"In the future, you and Jack will never travel together."

Malinda's eyes widened in surprise. "For heaven's sake, why?"

"I'm not taking any chances on the two of you dying in a plane crash or a car wreck and leaving the doctor here—" she said with a jerk of her head in Rand's direction "—and I in joint custody of all your kids. It would never work." She looked at Rand and shook her head, never more convinced of anything in her life. "Never," she repeated with conviction.

Rand stood at the nurse's station, ostensibly reviewing a chart with a nurse while keeping a watchful eye on Malinda's door, waiting for Cecile to appear. For a man who prided himself on never losing his temper, Rand Coursey was doing all he could not to spew steam.

It would never work. Never.

One side of his brain played back Cecile's words while the other absorbed the information the nurse was feeding him. Years spent training in stress-filled surgical suites had honed this ability razor sharp.

He wondered what made Cecile so damn sure their sharing godparent responsibilities for the Brannan children wouldn't work. He wasn't convinced, and he was a cautious man at best. There wasn't a man alive who spent more time weighing the angles of a situation before making a decision or drawing an opinion than Rand Coursey. As a result, once made, his stance on a matter was respected by those who knew him.

"And Mrs. Conradt in 202 is complaining about her episiotomy. Says the stitches are driving her crazy."

Rand started to respond, but at the same moment the door opened and Cecile appeared. He straightened, closing the chart, his eyes leveled on Cecile. Her gaze met his and quickly flitted away.

"Give Mrs. Conradt a sitz bath every four hours," he told the nurse, watching annoyance stain Cecile's neck red. "That should soothe the itching, but if it doesn't, page me."

He handed the chart to the nurse as Cecile marched past, looking everywhere but at him. Fully aware she'd resent his presence, he fell in beside her.

"Going home?" he asked, hiding his own irritation behind an affable smile.

"Yes." She punched the button for the elevator, then folded her arms at her breasts. Ignoring Rand, she lifted her gaze to watch the position indicator light as the car began its descent.

"May I treat you to a cup of coffee?"

The doors *shooshed* open. Cecile turned her head to look at him, a scowl gathering like a thundercloud on her forehead. "No," she said distinctly, then stepped aboard.

Rand moved in behind her. With a huff of impatience, Cecile edged to the handrail.

Pretending it was the coffee she was objecting to and not his company, he glanced at his watch. "It is a little late for coffee. How about a soda?"

"Take a hint, doctor," she said, her eyes glued to the position indicator. "I'm not interested." The light for the lobby blinked and the elevator door dinged open. Cecile strode out into lobby.

In two steps, Rand caught up with her and jerked her to a stop.

She dipped her head to frown at the hand clamped around her elbow. As surprised as she was by his he-man tactics, he released her. "I'd like to talk to you."

"Sorry, but I don't want to talk to you." She headed for the revolving doors at the entrance, dismissing him without a second glance.

A volunteer sat at the information desk, watching with interest the conversation taking place in front of her. Rand knew that by morning the hospital grapevine would be ripe with varying accounts of the scene Dr. Coursey had created in the lobby.

Fully aware of this, he yelled from behind Cecile, "Fine! Then I'll do all the talking."

Cecile paused long enough to shoot him a look, whose message was for him to travel to the point farthest south, before she gave the door an angry shove to start its slow turning.

When she stepped through into the humid night air on the other side, Rand was there waiting for her. Startled by his unexpected appearance, she glanced around just in time to see the handicapped access door slide back into place. Narrowing her eyes at him, she mumbled under her breath, "Figures," then shouldered her way past him.

Frustrated, Rand demanded, "What figures?"

"You cheated," she tossed over her shoulder as she skipped down the steps. "Must be a prerequisite to becoming a doctor or something. Or do they teach that in medical school, too?"

Scowling, he stuffed his hands into the pockets of his scrub pants to keep from strangling the aggravating woman, and followed her down the steps. "When are you going to quit blaming all men for one man's transgressions?"

Her key already fitted into the door lock of her Jeep Cherokee, Cecile wheeled, her eyes flashing. "I don't blame all men for anything, much less my deceased husband's transgressions."

"Then exactly what is it you have against me?"

Cecile sucked in a deep, shuddery breath and dropped her hand, leaving the key to dangle in the lock. "Personally, nothing. In general, everything." She turned her head to stare at the window of her vehicle, her lips firming into a thin, tight line. She cocked her head to look up at Rand, her eyes filled with an anger that took him totally by surprise. "My husband was a snake, doctor. He had affairs with more women than most men will meet in a lifetime, much less bed." She swung an arm in the direction of the hospital. "And that was his picking field. Nurses, aides, even wives and relatives of patients he was attending.

"I can't take a step inside that hospital without people staring at me. Some in pity. Others snickering behind my back. Every time I come face-to-face with a nurse or an aide, I can't help wondering if she might be one of the un- lucky ones who fell under Denton's spell." She took a step nearer Rand.

When her eyes met his in the glow of the parking lot's se- curity lights, she knew it was Rand Coursey she was look- ing at, but blinded by her anger, she saw only Denton Kingsley. Just like her husband, Rand used the title doctor to ingratiate himself with women. Hadn't he demonstrated as much earlier that day when he'd offered to pull rank on the nurses to get her into the nursery to see the twins?

And he had touched her. Freely. More than once. And with a smoothness that could only come with practice. A hand at the elbow, an arm draped around her shoulders. She'd caught her husband touching women in much the same way. When she'd confronted him, he'd told her she had an overactive imagination and that the situation was strictly innocent. Like a fool, she'd believed him.

Until she'd discovered her suspicions had been right on target.

As she glared at Rand, she told herself there wasn't a single thing about the man that appealed to her. Razor-cut hair—slightly mussed, for effect, she was sure—an ego bigger than Texas and an irresistible charm. She'd had a stomach full of just such a man and wasn't anxious to swallow any more of the same.

The fact that she'd felt the man's sexual pull, much less recognized it, made her turn away in disgust. "Never mind," she muttered, as she slammed the door of the Jeep behind her.

Rand stood in the parking lot, staring at her as she gunned the engine and backed out of the parking space with a squeal of tires. Long after the Jeep's rear lights had disappeared, he remained under the security light, staring after her, his mind clicking as he assembled and sorted data.

A little early to be sure, but in his estimation, Cecile Kingsley suffered from a very strong case of guilt, seeded by shame. It appeared she'd taken every sin her husband had ever committed and wore the guilt as if it were her own.

It was a pity, too. She was such an intriguing woman, full of spirit and life. The task would be a difficult one, but with a little patience and a whole lot of luck, he was convinced he could free her of her past and teach her how to love again.

If she'd let him. He shook his head as he turned back for the hospital's entrance. Getting close enough to help her would be a problem. She obviously didn't have a very high opinion of men . . . especially doctors.

Three

Cecile wrestled the heavy canvas bag of baseball equipment Jack had placed in the back of her Jeep to the open hatch, silently cursing her bad luck. To be required to share godparent responsibilities with Rand Coursey was one thing, but now it appeared she would be forced to share the coaching responsibilities of the team with the man, as well.

Okay, she conceded grudgingly, she understood Jack's position. With the arrival of the twins he *was* needed at home, but to arrange for Rand to take his place as coach without even asking her—well, that was just another indication of her bad luck.

She glanced over her shoulder to check the parking lot again. Empty. She gave the bag another angry tug. Figured. Doctors were the most unreliable men alive. How many times had Denton left her waiting? Too many to count, she reflected with a grunt and another tug. It appeared as if she'd have the responsibility of the team alone.

That thought drew a slow smile of revelation. Maybe her luck was changing, after all.

The bag finally gave and nearly knocked her down when it tumbled out of the Jeep and hit the ground with a thud. Baseballs bounced through the drawstring opening and rolled around her feet and beneath the Jeep.

Cecile heaved a frustrated sigh, dropped to her knees and started gathering them up. A car door slammed behind her. Assuming it was Joey, the team's relief pitcher who was always late, Cecile yelled as she ducked beneath the Jeep to snag a stray ball, "Hit the track with the rest of the guys and run laps. I'll holler when I have the field set up."

"Need any help?"

Cecile froze, flat on her stomach, her hand only inches from the ball. Just to make sure she hadn't mistaken the voice, she twisted her head around to look behind her. An adult-size pair of Reeboks and a pair of the cleanest athletic socks she'd seen outside a sporting goods store were all that were visible. But she knew who they belonged to and knew, too, that her luck had just run out. Dropping her face on the back of her dusty hand, she let out a resigned sigh.

Rand squatted down to peer under the Jeep. His view of Cecile was a little more revealing, consisting of the soles of a pair of tennies, a long stretch of tanned leg and the cutest swell of butt he'd ever seen fill a pair of athletic shorts.

Considering his busy schedule and his inexperience, he'd been hesitant at first in accepting Jack's invitation to replace him as baseball coach. But the offer was looking better all the time. Biting back a grin, he asked, "Are you stuck?"

Cecile's lips puckered in a frown against the back of her hands. "No, I'm not stuck."

"Need any help?"

"No, I don't need your help." She dug her toes in the ground and stretched to snag the ball. The effort inched up her shorts, exposing a glimpse of flexed butt muscles. Rand's brows shot up at the sight. He blew out a slow breath as he stood, giving Cecile room as she wriggled her way out.

Oblivious of the admiration warming Rand's eyes, she stood, slapped the ball in his hand, then bent to brush the dirt off her knees. "You're late. Practice starts at five-thirty."

Rand opened the bag and shoved the ball inside, ignoring her accusatory tone. "Sorry, Coach, but rounds at the hospital ran long." He swung the bag over his shoulder, slipped his other arm around Cecile and headed her toward the diamond. "So, what's the game plan?"

Without missing a step, Cecile picked up his hand and lifted it off her shoulder, using two fingers as if handling a dead, smelly fish.

"The plan is to teach these boys how to play baseball, and in the process, hopefully win a few games." When she reached the dugout, she took the bag from him and started shaking out equipment. "Jack usually worked with the infield and the pitchers, while I worked the outfield and gave the boys some batting practice. Joey, the relief pitcher, is having trouble with his curve, so when he gets here, you'll need to help him with it." She tossed him a glove.

Rand caught it, frowning.

"Do you have a problem?" she asked.

"Well . . ." He lowered his gaze to the glove as he worked it back and forth between his hands.

Exasperated, Cecile cried, "Well, what?"

"I don't know how to throw a curve ball."

Rolling her eyes, she turned and headed for right field. "Work on his fast ball, then."

"Cecile?"

She stopped and turned. "What now?"

"I don't know how to throw a fast ball, either."

"Do you know anything about pitching?" she cried in disbelief. When his forehead puckered into the beginnings of a frown, Cecile waved the question away with her hand. "Never mind, never mind." She marched back and picked up a bat. "You do know what a bat is, don't you?"

Rand tried hard not to smile. "Yes, as a matter of fact, I do."

"Can you hit flys and skinners to the outfielders?"

Rand grinned. "You bet."

She threw the bat at him. He caught it before it knocked him in the head. "Then do it!" she snapped.

Rand continued to grin as he watched her flounce away, slapping a glove against her thigh and mumbling something about idiots and playboys.

He was going to have to remember to send Jack a bottle of wine in thanks for letting him fill in as coach. His summer was looking better and better all the time.

Cecile squinted up at the sun as she swiped her arm at the sweat beading her forehead. It had to be a hundred degrees. She was hot, sweaty, irritable and would have traded her firstborn for something cool to drink. But there was still thirty minutes of practice remaining.

"Okay, boys, gather round." She motioned them to stand in a loose horseshoe around home plate, leaving the third base line open. "The last game we played, you guys seemed to have a problem sliding, so we're going to work on that for a while."

She glanced up at Rand, the perpetual frown she'd worn all afternoon deepening. "Dr. Coursey will be the catcher, and I'll be the runner coming into home plate. We'll run through it once, demonstrating how it's done, then you guys can each have a try." She eyed Rand warily. "Ready?"

He socked his fist into the catcher's mitt and gave her a confident smile. "You bet, Coach. Ready when you are." He took his position in front of home plate while Cecile jogged about three-quarters of the way to third base. Turning, she bent over, hands on knees, getting a bead on Rand and the plate.

"Remember, boys," she warned. "Sliding can be dangerous if not executed properly. Charge as fast as you can for the catcher, keeping an eye on his glove. Just before you reach him, drop to your left hip, left leg curled, right toe stretching for the plate and slide. Got it?" she asked as she dug her toe into the baseline, preparing herself for the run.

"Got it, Coach," they echoed.

Poised in a runner's crouch, she sprinted for home plate, gaining speed, her arms pumping, her legs churning, her gaze focused on the glove and ball in Rand's hand. About two feet short of him, she dropped to her hip and slid.

What happened next, Cecile couldn't exactly say. Dust billowed around her, choking and blinding her; then her foot hit what felt like a brick wall. She cried out when her ankle wrenched, but then a dead weight hit her right smack in the chest, knocking the breath from her.

Flat on her back, her ankle throbbing, her eyes bugged wide as she struggled to suck in much-needed air, she looked up into the grinning face of Rand Coursey.

"You're out!" he pronounced proudly, hitching himself up and away to stand over her. He stretched out a hand to help her up. When she didn't take it, the smile slowly melted off his face. "You okay?" he asked, dropping to a knee at her side.

Her mouth open, sucking at air that wouldn't pass the wall blocking her throat, Cecile simply stared at him.

"Get me the water jug and a towel," Rand ordered the boy closest to him.

He lifted Cecile's upper body and rested her head on his knee, hoping to ease her attempts to breathe. The water jug bumped his knee and a towel was shoved into his hand. Tipping the container, he poured water onto the cloth, then bathed the dirt and sweat from Cecile's forehead and face. Eleven nine-year-olds hovered around them like vultures over a ripe carcass.

He soothed her with words as well as with his hand as he tried to calm her, knowing if she'd quit fighting for breath and just let it fill her, she'd be breathing again in no time.

"Did you kill her?" a small voice asked from just beyond his elbow.

Rand glanced over and straight into the fear-filled but accusing gaze of Dent Kingsley, Cecile's oldest son. "No, I didn't kill her," he replied, though he felt very much like a mass murderer. "Just knocked the breath out of her."

"Will she be okay?" he persisted.

"Yes, she—"

Cecile pushed to a sitting position, flapping a feeble hand in the direction of her son and silencing Rand. "I'm... f-f-fine," she gasped, pressing a hand to her chest as the first breath eased into her burning lungs. She struggled to her feet, not wanting to frighten the boys any more than they already were.

But when her right foot hit the ground, she crumpled against Rand's side, clinging to him for support. "My ankle," she moaned against the soft cotton at his shoulder, hoping to hide her pain from the boys. "I think it's broken."

Not giving her time to argue the point, as he knew she probably would, Rand scooped her up into his arms and carried her to the bench in the dugout, shadowed by the boys. After settling her on the bench, he knelt in front of her and cradled her right foot in his hand. Gently he ran his fingers over the injured ankle, making Cecile suck in a tortured breath. She dropped her head back against the chain-link fence behind her, her face pale, her lips pressed tight over clenched teeth.

"Nothing broken. Just a sprain." He motioned Dent to his side. "Get a handful of ice from the cooler and we'll fill her sock with it to cut down on the swelling."

"What's going on? A strategy meeting?" Jack Brannan's long shadow fell over Rand's hand.

Rand looked up, his hand curved protectively around Cecile's ankle. "No, an injured player," he replied miserably.

With a speed and understanding that Rand would thank him for later, Jack quickly assessed the situation and began herding the boys out of the dugout. "Come on guys, some of your parents are waiting. Let's gather up the equipment and I'll walk you to the parking lot."

Feeling responsible as hell for hurting Cecile, Rand sighed as he turned back to pack the ice around her swollen ankle. "I'm sorry, Cecile. I guess I was a little rough."

The touch of ice against her bare leg had Cecile tensing and shrinking away. But it was the contrasts between the cold cubes and the heat of Rand's hand that sent shivers racing down her spine. "It's okay," she said on a strangled breath, her gaze fixed on the top of his bent head. She was amazed that a part of her wished he'd drop the ice and wrap his soothing hands around her ankle again.

As if she'd voiced the request aloud, he returned his hands to her leg and moved them in a gentle massage around the lower portion of her leg, while he kept her foot propped in the V of his lap.

"No, it's not okay," he said, his voice filled with self-condemnation. "I was so determined to prove to you that I could be useful, I came on a little too strong." He lifted his head, revealing brown eyes filled with remorse. "It's all my fault, and I'm sorry."

The statement made her forget how soothing the feel of his hands were on her leg, and Cecile could only stare. Nothing in her previous experience with men had prepared her for this. Raised with three brothers, the only apologies she'd ever received from them were those demanded by her parents and, when offered, sounded more like a threat than an apology. As for her husband, he'd never apologized for anything, whether responsible for the wrong or not.

Uncomfortable with this unfamiliar side of a man, she shifted on the bench. "Really, Rand, it's okay. You played the position well." She managed a small chuckle. "To be honest, better than I expected. I never dreamed you'd try to stop me from sliding past you into home."

"Everybody all right in here?"

Cecile lifted her head to see Jack standing in the dugout opening. "Everyone's fine," she said, relieved by his presence.

"Need some help getting home?"

Cecile started to respond, but Rand turned to Jack, blocking her view of him. "I'll take her, but I might need you to follow me back over here later and pick up my car."

"I'll be at home. Just give me a call." He turned to Cecile. "Are Gordy and CeeCee at your mother's?"

"Yes."

"I'll drop Dent by there and tell her what happened. Knowing your mother, I'm sure she'll insist on them spending the night with her."

Cecile sighed, for Jack had pegged her mother right. She was always looking for an excuse to keep her three grandchildren, and tonight she definitely wouldn't get an argument from Cecile. "Without a doubt. Thanks, Jack."

"No problem. You just stay off that foot."

Finding herself alone again with Rand, Cecile couldn't think of a single thing to say. His hands remained on her calf, her foot propped in his lap. The intimacy of that position became as awkward as the silence, and Cecile felt heat creep up her neck.

She clapped her palms against her thighs. "Well!" she exclaimed on a forced note of cheerfulness. "Guess we better head for home."

Carefully, Rand lowered her foot to the ground and pressed his hands to his knees as he stood. Bending, he hoisted Cecile from the bench and into his arms before she knew his intent.

She tried to wriggle free. "This isn't necessary, Rand. I can walk."

He stopped and looked down at her, the intensity of his gaze making her go still. "And I can carry you, so humor me."

"Do you have a heating pad?"

Cecile stifled a groan. What would he think of next? She'd suffered about all the coddling she could stomach for one day.

The drive home had been a test of endurance. Just to make sure he didn't jostle her around too much, Rand had driven at a speed that would make an old geezer out for a Sunday drive look like Mario Andretti. And if that wasn't bad enough, he'd insisted on carrying her into the house, tucking her into bed, fluffing pillows behind her back and under her foot and making an ice pack to place on her elevated foot.

She'd already decided if he offered her chicken soup, she'd pour it over his head. Maybe then he'd get the message. She didn't need or want his pampering!

"No," she lied, hoping that with nothing left for him to do, he'd leave. "I don't have a heating pad."

"I'll run to the drugstore and buy one."

He was already fishing the keys out of his pocket before Cecile could stop him.

"Wait!" she cried, pretending she'd just remembered owning one. "I think I do. Look in the linen closet in the hallway."

Thirty seconds later, Rand was returning with the heating pad and unwrapping its cord to plug it into the outlet beside her bed. Gently he lifted her foot, removed the ice pack and settled the pad around her ankle. The cushion hadn't had time to warm, yet heat crawled from her ankle to knot in her abdomen. Trying to ignore the effect his touch had on her, she focused on his movements.

The hands that moved over her were wide and strong, the backs of which were dusted with light brown hair. Long, blunt-tipped fingers moved skillfully and methodically over her skin. Denton's hands had been similar, but Rand's were somehow different. Cecile frowned as she tried to put her finger on exactly what that difference was.

Kind.

The word jumped out at her, and she flinched as if she'd been slapped. That was it. Though he moved with an efficiency and competency not unlike Denton's, Rand's touch was kind and nurturing where Denton's had always been cool and indifferent.

"We'll need to alternate cold and heat about every fifteen minutes or so to control the swelling," he said as he rolled his fist in the pillow to make a nest for her foot.

Cecile thought she'd surely drown in sugary sweet syrup or else be tempted to clone him and pass him out to her single friends if he did one more helpful thing. When he reached to fluff the pillows behind her head, she clamped her hand over his wrist. "Rand, really, you've done enough."

Slowly, he withdrew.

Not wanting to offend him—after all, he'd done everything within his power to make up for the pain he'd caused—she offered him a grateful smile. "I appreciate all you've done, but enough's enough. Go home."

"But you can't walk. What if you need something?"

"I assure you, I don't need a thing. But if I do, I'll call Mother or Malinda."

She could tell by the stubborn look on his face, she was going to have to convince him. She sweetened the smile. "Before you go, though, would you mind getting me a glass of water from the kitchen? That and a couple of aspirin and I'll be settled for the night."

"I'll get the aspirin, but I'm not leaving."

Cecile hid her exasperation behind a submissive nod of acceptance. "Whatever you think best."

As soon as he was out of sight, Cecile whipped open the bedside table drawer and tugged out the telephone directory, grumbling under her breath. Quickly finding the number she wanted, she punched it in and waited for the answering service to respond.

"Dr. Coursey's service. May I help you?"

"Yes," she moaned, trying to sound out of breath and in pain. "I'm a patient of Dr. Coursey's and I'm in labor. The contractions are three minutes apart. Have him meet me at Mercy Hospital as soon as possible." She slammed down the receiver before the woman could ask her name.

Rand called from the kitchen, "Where do you keep the aspirin?"

"In the cabinet by the sink, top shelf," she yelled back, then twisted to shove the telephone directory back in the drawer before he returned and caught her.

Beep. Beep. Beep.

Silently laughing, Cecile fell back against the pillows.

Rand hurried into the room, juggling a glass of water and a bottle of aspirin. "My service just paged. One of my patients is in labor. I'm going to have to run. I hope it's all right if I borrow your car. Is there anything else I can get you before I leave?"

Cecile accepted the glass and the aspirin bottle he shoved at her, trying her darnedest to look innocent. "No, I'm fine."

He was already turning for the bedroom door. "I'll check on you later," he said over his shoulder.

"Don't bother," she called after him. "I'm all settled for the night. But thanks, Rand."

When she heard the back door slam, she sat up with a jerk. At last, she was rid of him. Dragging her elbows through her T-shirt's armholes, she unhooked her bra, slipped it off, then paused long enough to let out a sigh of relief before poking her arms back through the shirt openings. Bras had never been high on her list of necessary wear for women, and she wouldn't be wearing one now if her mother hadn't insisted it proper for a woman of her age.

Lifting her hips, she shoved her shorts to her knees, then bit her lip as she eased them over her swollen ankle. Sighing her contentment, she tossed the shorts to the floor, snuggled down into her pillows and closed her eyes, praying that by morning her ankle would be as good as new.

Rand turned into Cecile's driveway, still puzzling over the fact that one of his patients hadn't been admitted to the hospital. He'd waited more than an hour, double checking with his service, just to make sure the woman who'd called hadn't phoned again to say her labor was a false alarm.

Prank calls weren't unusual. Rand had received his share, but his service had been so sure this call was on the up-and-up, saying the woman had sounded frightened and in pain.

Shaking his head, he took Cecile's key ring and flipped his way through it, trying to decide which one looked like a house key as he headed for the back door. His third attempt proved correct and the knob twisted in his hand.

He stuck his head in the door and listened, but not a sound greeted him. Tiptoeing across the brick kitchen floor, he called softly, "Cecile?"

Not receiving a reply, he continued down the hall to her bedroom. The bedside lamp was off, but moonlight slanted through plantation shutters, offering just enough illumination to make out her huddled form on the bed. Again guilt stabbed at him as he remembered the way she'd looked when he'd left her. Her face pale, her mouth pinched against the pain, and an ankle swollen to twice its normal size.

Easing to the side of the bed, he reached out a hand to switch on the light so he could check her ankle to see if the swelling had gone down.

A woman all too aware of her responsibilities as the only adult in a house of four, Cecile had learned over the years to sleep with one ear cocked and one eye open. So it was no surprise that when the back door hinges squeaked, her eyes blinked open and she stared into the darkness, listening.

Muffled footsteps coming down the hallway had her struggling to a sitting position. A stabbing pain in her ankle made her wilt back against her pillow, stifling a moan. She lay there a moment, then firmed her lips and eased her hand beneath the mattress. Her fingers settled on what she fondly referred to as her "friend," a lethal-looking billy club.

She saw the shadow first and knew without a doubt her prowler was a man. Remaining motionless, feigning sleep, she tightened her fingers on the billy club, waiting as the shadow took form and the prowler inched his way to the bed.

The minute he lifted his hand, Cecile let out a yell Gordy's karate instructor would have been proud of and swung with all her weight. The club hit the side of the man's head with a resounding *crack!* She watched, her heart lodged tight in her throat as the dark figure staggered, stumbling back a step, then forward two, before pitching full-length across her lap.

His upper body pinned her at the waist and thighs. Repulsed more than afraid, she tried to wriggle from beneath his dead weight, but discovered she couldn't move an inch. The man weighed what felt like a ton, and the slightest movement had her ankle throbbing unbearably.

"Oh, God, now what do I do?" She bit her lower lip, her eyes locked on the black lump stretched across her, watching for any sign of movement as she tried to come up with a plan.

A weapon. She had to see if he had a weapon. Stretching to the limit, she managed to switch on the bedside lamp. Twisting back around, she sucked in a sharp breath as her eyes took in the profile of Rand Coursey.

"Oh, dear God," she whispered against fingers pressed tightly to her lips. "I've killed him."

Tentatively, fearful of what her fingers might discover, she leaned to place a trembling hand at his throat. She held her breath as she gently searched for a pulse. When she found it, she sagged forward, her forehead resting in the crook of her elbow, her breath escaping on a sigh of relief. He was still breathing.

But if she was any judge, he'd have one heck of a headache when he regained consciousness.

Biting her lower lip, she leaned back against her pillows to wait. Seconds seemed like hours as she watched, silently praying for him to move. When at last he did, the guttural groan that rumbled from deep within him had Cecile biting harder at her lip.

Cautiously she leaned toward him, combing his hair back so she could see the lump already forming at his hairline. "Rand?" she whispered. "Rand? Are you okay?"

Slowly his hand came up to touch his temple. Wincing, he rolled to his back and groaned. "What happened?" he asked, his voice husky.

"Well—I sort of hit you."

He cocked his head, narrowing an eye at her. "*Sort of* hit me?"

She tried to smile. "Yeah. I thought you were a prowler."

"What'd you hit me with, a sledgehammer?"

Chuckling, Cecile replied, "No. Just my friend." She lifted the billy club for him to see. "My younger brother, Tony, is a cop, and after Denton died, he insisted I have a gun. I was afraid to keep it in the house because of the kids, so he gave me this instead."

Dubiously, Rand eyed the deadly looking club, then dropped his head back, covering his eyes with a hand. "Thank God you didn't keep the gun." He lay there a moment, trying to find the strength to rise. If he hadn't been afraid his head would fall off at the exertion, he might have laughed. To think he'd raced to her house from the hospital to make sure she was all right. As if the woman needed someone to take care of her.

That realization was almost as debilitating to his ego as the rap against his head had been to his body.

Feeling useless and more than a little foolish, he pushed to an elbow. "I guess I'll be going." Darkness threatened and slowly he sank back, pressing his hands at his temples. His head throbbed, his ears rang and every joint in his body felt as if the bone had been replaced with peanut butter.

Not one who handled sickness well, Cecile watched his face whiten, her own stomach knotting convulsively. "You aren't going to throw up, are you?"

Rand groaned. "No," he murmured, not at all sure he wasn't about to be sick but too embarrassed by his weakness to admit it.

"Sometimes a person does when they receive a head injury."

"Yes, I know."

Cecile squirmed until she'd freed her legs from beneath his weight. She ignored the pain in her ankle as she moved to kneel over him. "Can I do anything?"

"No, you've done enough."

"But surely there's something—"

"No," he said firmly, then, more gently, "Just be still for a minute until my head stops spinning, then I'll go home."

She remembered the ice pack Rand had prepared for her ankle and dug around in the tangle of bed covers for it. "Here, this will help the swelling." She laid it at his temple and pressed.

Flinching at the sting of cold, Rand reached up and placed his hand over hers, adjusting the bag to a more bearable position. Though most of the ice had melted, the bag was still cold enough to accomplish its purpose. With a sigh, Rand relaxed, closing his eyes and allowing the ice to work its wonders on his throbbing head.

The fact that Rand's hand remained on hers over the ice pack didn't go unnoticed by Cecile, but at the moment she was more concerned for his welfare and the knot on his head than she was about his touch. She sat as still as a mouse and watched his face. Gradually the color returned to his cheeks. She breathed a sigh of relief, but remained watchful.

After a while, prickles of pain at her ankle had her easing her feet out from under her. With no other space available to her, she stretched out beside Rand, one hand holding the ice pack in place while she propped her head in the palm of the other.

The position put her face at a level just above his head. From her angle, she could see the rhythmic rise and fall of his chest and assumed he must have dozed off. She fought back a grin. Doctors were notorious for their uncanny ability to close their eyes and instantly sleep. She supposed the trick was learned during their medical training when rest had to be snatched in stolen minutes rather than hours. Knowing he'd be more comfortable sleeping off the pain than dealing with it awake, she let him sleep.

Moisture from the ice pack beaded on the skin below his temple, and Cecile leaned to carefully wipe it away before it rivered down his neck. When her fingers met his damp skin, she winced at the size of the knot. Angling her hand, she stroked a gentle finger over the egg-shaped lump while remorse that she was responsible for it thickened in her throat. He moaned softly and turned his cheek into her palm.

Cecile's eyebrows shot up in alarm as he nestled his cheek in the cradle of her hand. The movement spoke of an intimacy, a familiarity that had Cecile tensing. In spite of her determination to repel it, the rasp of five o'clock shadow chafing against her soft skin sent lightning bolts of sensations shooting through her. Not daring to move, much less breathe, she waited until he grew still again. Unable to believe such a simple movement on his part could have such a devastating effect on her, she eased closer to stare at his face in the soft lamplight.

Thick, dark lashes fringed his eyes and feathered cheekbones slashed high and stained a healthy pink. The slightly parted lips, the rhythmic breathing, convinced her he slept and his movements were innocent, not part of some concocted seduction scheme.

Though she tried hard to control the urge, Cecile found her gaze slipping down the length of his body. Broad shoulders, tapered waist, muscled thighs and calves. Though he was anything but athletic in her estimation, he had one heck of a physique, and she couldn't help but wonder what he did to maintain it.

Returning her gaze to his face, she slowly released a pent-up breath. Asleep he looked boyish, innocent—but then, didn't all men? Cecile frowned at the thought. She'd learned never to be fooled by looks alone. She'd also learned—the hard way—to mistrust a man's actions. Denton had taught her that men were consummate actors and could project any image they desired to get what they wanted.

Reminding herself of this, she closed her eyes against Rand's handsomeness, her own curiosity and the ball of attraction that had gelled like warm, thick honey in her most secret parts. She rested her head against her arm, mentally steeling herself against the comforting warmth and reassurance of the body lying so close to hers.

She wouldn't be sucked in by a man's charm. Not again.

Four

A solitary man who had formed his own set of exacting habits over the years, Rand Coursey commonly slept on his back. Sprawled across the length of his king-size bed, he demanded—and received, since there was no one to argue the point—the lion's share of the space. Invariably upon awakening, he'd find the fingertips of his left hand tucked just beneath the elastic waist of a pair of paisley, silk boxer shorts, while his right hand cupped the base of his neck.

Considering this, he was surprised to awaken on this particular morning cramped, lying on his side, his head cradled in the crook of his right arm while his left lay in the sensuous curve of a woman's waist. A bared and decidedly aroused nipple nudged at the palm of his hand. Lying with her back to his front, the woman had curled her buttocks into his groin and was moving her hips in a slow, sinuous circuit.

Most surprising of all to Rand was that he found the sensation not in the least bit unpleasant. In fact, he discovered his own body had responded to her movements, leaving him rock hard and wanting.

Baffled by these bizarre deviations from his normal morning routine, he blinked open his eyes to find his view blocked by a tangle of honey blond hair. Brushing it aside, he leaned to peer over the woman's shoulder. His eyes widened in shock. Though the woman was asleep and only half her face was visible, he recognized her immediately.

Cecile Kingsley.

Remembering the previous evening's events, he slowly lowered his head back to the crook of his arm and closed his eyes, groaning. It was the rap on the head, he told himself. Cecile Kingsley had made her position on men perfectly clear. She hated them, especially doctors. There was no way on earth this woman would willingly be curled up in a bed with him. He had to be suffering some form of delusion as a result of the head injury.

To test his sensibilities, he methodically named all the bones in the body, beginning with the phalanges and ending with the cranium. He then mentally listed the Periodic Table of Chemical Elements from hydrogen to lawrencium, naming their atomic numbers, symbols and atomic weights, as well.

Satisfied that he was alert and in full control of his mental faculties, he slowly opened his eyes only to find it wasn't a delusion. Cecile Kingsley still lay curled seductively in front of him. He let out a slow, shaky breath as her hips continued to move in that slow sensuous grind against his hardness.

He couldn't take much more of this pain-pleasure and knew he should tell her to stop before things got totally out of hand . . . but damn, she felt good.

* * *

As the first glimmerings of dawn pinkened the sky, Cecile stirred. Desire, bold and insistent, had already carved a hollow sensation low in her abdomen. Lust-filled cravings clawed at its edges, demanding immediate and pleasure-releasing satisfaction.

More asleep than awake, she snuggled against the shaft of hardness cradled against her buttocks and purred like a cream-sated cat. Stretching her toes out, she curled her foot around a muscular calf and drew the warm mass of maleness behind her closer still. The prod of manhood against her silk panties was both exciting and frustrating.

While she measured his level of arousal with her hips, his lips, warm and moist, found the sensitive skin behind her ear and nibbled a path down her neck. She softly moaned her appreciation as she arched, offering him easier access.

Warming her skin with his breath, her early-morning lover nudged aside the soft fabric of her T-shirt and continued his sensuous journey across her shoulder. The sensation charged her body with millions of electrifying tingles.

A woman who appreciated and enjoyed an active sex life, Cecile didn't find her current hunger in any way out of the ordinary or alarming ... until she remembered with whom she shared her bed.

Stiffening, she flipped open her eyes and slowly turned her head, just to be sure.

His lips still pressed at her bare shoulder, Rand lifted his gaze to warm her with soft bedroom eyes. Slowly, holding her enraptured with his gaze, he pulled his lips from their sensuous journey. He grinned a slow, lusty smile.

"Good morning," he murmured.

His words broke the spell he held over Cecile. "What in the hell do you think you're doing?" she demanded angrily. Before he could reply, she shoved his hand from her breast, tugged down her T-shirt and pivoted away from him. Clamoring to her knees, she spun to face him.

Rand's smile disappeared and his eyes narrowed. "Giving you what you asked for."

"I didn't ask to be pawed by you," she cried indignantly, crossing her arms beneath her breasts.

He raised himself to an elbow, his motions slow and lazy, defying the anger that heated his own blood. "Not verbally, but your body certainly sent out its own request."

"Oh? And what request was that?" she demanded, incensed that he'd think she wanted anything from him except distance.

Rand pursed his lips and arched a brow her way. "Need I be specific?"

"Yes, you do," she replied acidly. "I certainly wouldn't want my body to make that mistake again."

Rand heaved a frustrated breath. He didn't want to argue with her, he wanted to make love with her and ease this ache she'd created within him. But obviously Cecile's past experience with her husband had left her scarred and unable to deal with the physical demands of her own body.

"Cecile," he said patiently, "sexuality is nothing to be ashamed of or alarmed by. The physical attraction between a man and woman can be both healthy and enjoyable if handled in a mature and responsible manner."

Cecile simply stared at him, her chin dropping. Then she laughed. Not the ladylike or self-conscious little giggle Rand might have suspected from another woman in similar circumstances, but a side-splitting, knee-slapping howl.

"Did I say something funny?" he asked, offended by her reaction.

Still laughing, Cecile batted a feeble hand at him. "No. No, it's just that you've got me pegged all wrong. For some strange reason, you think I don't like sex." She edged off the bed, still chuckling as she scraped her tangled hair back from her face. "That isn't the case at all."

She stood for a moment, looking at him, her face still flushed with passion but her eyes alight with humor. "For your information, Dr. Coursey, I enjoy a very healthy sex life." To his surprise, and without further explanation, she turned and limped away, leaving Rand alone in the bed.

At the bathroom doorway, though, she paused and cocked her head to look back over her shoulder at him. She added demurely, "I'm just very selective about who I choose for a lover. And you, Dr. Coursey, don't qualify."

From his position behind home plate, Rand had a perfect view of Cecile and the four players she was working with out in center field. As he watched her pitch to one of the boys, he frowned. He was still irritated with her. Even after four days in which to cool off. Rejection wasn't something he'd had much experience with—at least, not until he'd met Cecile—and he was having a heck of a time dealing with it now.

To further irritate him, every time she bent to scoop a ball from the field, her athletic shorts rode up, exposing a swell of paler skin he'd have to be blind to miss. He also couldn't help noticing how her sweat-dampened T-shirt clung to her skin, further emphasizing the fact that today, of all days, she'd chosen not to wear a bra. She was doing it all on purpose, just to rub his nose in her sexuality, hoping, he was sure, he'd come begging for more of her rejections.

"Okay, boys, take a breather!" Cecile dropped her glove by the pile of balls in the grass and jogged toward Rand, while the boys ran to join the other players by the cooler of water.

Not wanting her to think he'd been watching her, Rand immediately busied himself kicking dirt around home plate, smoothing out the hills and valleys created by the boys' cleats.

"Joey's not here yet?" she asked as she approached.

"No," he mumbled as he continued to kick dirt, pretending to ignore her.

Cecile stopped at his side and put her hands on her hips. Catching her bottom lip between her teeth, she worriedly cast her gaze toward the empty parking lot. "He's always late, but it's not like him to totally miss practice." She glanced at Rand, a frown furrowing her brow. "Did any of the guys say anything about him?"

"No," he said, further humiliated to see that her attention had been on one of the players and not on him. "Nobody said a word. He probably just forgot."

"No," Cecile replied, shaking her head. "Joey never forgets practice." She stood a moment, shifting her weight from one foot to the other, and continued to watch the empty parking lot.

Rand glanced at his watch. "It's already nearly six-thirty. If he was coming, he'd be here by now."

"I know. That's what has me worried."

The look of distress on her face had Rand forgetting his anger with her and his determination to ignore her. "Is there a problem here? Something I should be aware of?"

"Well—" Cecile tore her gaze from the parking lot and turned it on Rand. "Maybe. I'm not sure."

The look of fear in her eyes had Rand grabbing her elbow and dragging her to the dugout and out of hearing range of the players. After pushing her onto the wooden bench, he sat down bedside her. "Okay. Give it to me straight. All of it."

She hesitated a moment, then reluctantly complied. "I haven't mentioned it because I don't have any proof. Just my suspicions." She took a deep breath and plunged in.

"Joey's parents are divorced, and he lives with his mother. She has a new boyfriend that she seems pretty serious about, which would be great, except the guy doesn't seem to like kids much."

Sensing there was more to the story, Rand said, "And?"

"And I think the guy has taken a few punches at Joey," she said in a rush. She bolted to her feet and paced to the end of the dugout, as if to escape the ugliness of what she'd just revealed.

"How do you know this?"

She wheeled to face him, concern for the child turning her blue eyes misty. "I don't for sure, but Joey's come to practice a couple of times with bruises on his arms and face. When I asked him about them, he mumbled something about being clumsy and falling down."

Not wanting to accept Cecile's assumptions, Rand said hopefully, "Maybe he's telling the truth."

Cecile glared at him. "And what if he's not?"

A sick feeling churned in Rand's stomach at the thought. Dark, shadowed memories of his own childhood pushed at his consciousness, but he shoved them back. Abruptly he stood. "Until he asks for help, there's nothing we can do." He turned away, hoping to put an end to the discussion.

"But what if he needs help at this very minute and can't ask for it?"

Rand stopped, curled his fingers in the chain-link fence surrounding the dugout, and looked out at the parking lot where parents were starting to arrive to pick up their sons. A frown turned the corners of his mouth down into a scowl.

Under any other circumstances, Rand would have charged in, offering his assistance to the person in need—but this particular burden Rand didn't want. One look at Cecile's face, though, convinced him he couldn't walk away.

"If it'll make you feel better, I'll drive by his house and check on him on my way home." He brushed past Cecile, but she caught his elbow before he could escape.

"Thanks, Rand."

The touch of her fingers on his skin did funny things to his ability to breathe. "No problem," he mumbled, anxious to get away from her.

Her face brightened. "If he's there, why don't you invite him over to my house for dinner? We're going to cook hamburgers on the grill, and the two of you could join us."

He stared at her a moment, dreading the confrontation awaiting him at Joey's house for reasons he couldn't share with Cecile. But maybe she was right. Maybe if he checked on Joey, he could find out the truth behind the bruises. And if what Cecile suspected was true, Joey might need the company and distraction of boys his own age.

But if he accepted her invitation, he'd have to deal with her...or himself, he wasn't sure which. The plight of the boy won out over his own desire to avoid an evening filled with Cecile's own special form of torture.

"Okay," he conceded. "If he's there and his mom agrees."

The directions Cecile gave Rand led him to an older neighborhood within walking distance of downtown Edmond. Most of the homes were frame, but seemingly well-maintained. Crape myrtles, weighted down with heavy pink blooms, adorned most of the lawns. An occasional cottonwood towered above a roof line, promising the kids in the neighborhood an island of shade and a patch of bare ground on which to shoot marbles or the breeze, whichever struck their fancy.

A knot of nostalgia tightened Rand's chest. He himself had spent his early years in just such a neighborhood. From

May through August, he and his buddies would run bare-foot through the streets, playing hide-and-seek and catching fireflies in old mason jars. An easy, carefree life—until his stepfather had appeared on the scene.

The muscles in his face rigid, Rand wheeled his car to the curb in front of Joey's house and took three slow, deep breaths. He couldn't change his own past, but he might be able to make Joey's childhood a little sweeter. Even though that goal was noble and one Rand truly wanted to see achieved, he had to force himself to climb from the car and walk up the sidewalk leading to the house.

A glance toward the drive revealed no car and renewed Rand's hope that Cecile's assumptions were wrong. Maybe Joey and his mother were just off somewhere on an errand or visiting friends. As he stepped up onto the porch, he noticed that the drapes on the front windows of the house were closed tight.

He lifted a fist to the door, convinced no one was home and he'd been saved the confrontation. He was turning away when he heard a muffled voice ask, "Who's there?"

He recognized Joey's youthful voice immediately. "Dr. Coursey, Joey. May I come in?"

The door opened a crack, but the boy remained in the shadows. "My mom said to not let in any strangers."

"Good advice and very wise of you to heed it, but I'm not a stranger. I'm your baseball coach, so that means I'm not a stranger, right, Joey?"

The door opened a few more inches, revealing a darkened living room with no light other than that produced by the flicker of a television screen. "Yeah, I guess. What do you want?"

The boy sounded nervous, as if he were trying to hide something. For the kid's sake, as well as his own, Rand hoped he wasn't. Though Rand squinted hard against the darkness, he couldn't see more than the shadowed shape of Joey's form. "You missed practice and I came by to check on you, make sure you weren't sick or something."

"Nah, I'm not sick. Just didn't have a ride."

"Doesn't your mother usually bring you?"

"Yeah, but she and Dave—well, they had plans, so I'm stuck at home."

"Oh." Rand stood a moment, shifting uncomfortably, remembering times he'd been left at home alone. He wanted to push for more information, but feared he'd scare the boy into silence. "You know, Joey, it wouldn't be out of my way to stop by and pick you up on my way to practice."

Joey looked at him suspiciously. "You'd do that?"

"Sure, any time. Just give me a call."

"Okay, if I need one," he replied, still looking doubtful.

"Have you had dinner yet?"

"Nah," he said as he screwed up his nose. "Mom left a TV dinner, but I hate chicken pot pie."

Rand chuckled. "Not a personal favorite of mine, either. Tell you what. Cecile's cooking hamburgers on the grill and said for me to bring you along. Do you think your mom would mind?"

Joey threw the door wide and leapt onto the porch. "Heck, no! I'll just leave a note on the refrigerator."

Rand found himself standing alone on the driveway, staring after Dent and Joey as they disappeared around the back of Cecile's house. The resilience of youth. He shook his head at his own fears and misgivings. If Joey were suffering any physical or emotional damage at the hand of his mother's boyfriend, he was hiding it well, for Rand had all but put the kid under a light and found nothing to be concerned about.

Thank God.

Rand lifted his nose and sniffed the evening air. The enticing scent of meat grilling over mesquite wood made his mouth water in anticipation. He took a step in the direction Dent and Joey had disappeared, but jerked to a stop when he heard a hair-raising yell followed by a deafening cacophony of voices.

Judging by the noise level, there had to be a hundred kids playing in Cecile's backyard. Rand was tempted to climb back into his car and drive away before Cecile spotted him, but before he could retreat, he heard a sniffle.

Turning, he saw a little girl pushing a wobbly baby carriage down the sidewalk in front of Cecile's house. The child's head was down, her sandals scuffing dejectedly against the pebbled concrete. Chubby little legs extended from a bright yellow sundress while an off-center part divided a mass of curly blond hair into two slightly lopsided pigtails.

She glanced up, revealing tear-filled blue eyes set in the most cherubic face. When she saw Rand, a smile bloomed, deepening dimples on her cheeks. She charged forward, pushing the teetering baby carriage toward him.

"Hi! Are you Dr. Coursey? Mama said I was supposed to watch for you and bring you around back when you got here." She jerked the carriage to a stop just short of running over his feet. "Are you gonna eat with us? We're having hamburgers and chips and baked beans, and there's a watermelon iced down in the cooler on the patio. Want to see it?"

Grinning, Rand dropped to one knee. "Yes, I'm Dr. Coursey. And, yes, I'm going to eat with you. And, yes," he said, chuckling, "I'd love to see the watermelon." He lifted a finger and wiped a tear from her cheek. "But first, tell me your name."

"CeeCee."

"Why the tears, CeeCee?"

Her smile melted into a pout. "The boys won't play with me. They called me a baby." She dipped her head and stubbed the toe of her sandal against a raised pebble on the drive.

He eyed her a moment, his heart melting. "You don't look like a baby to me."

She slowly lifted her head, her eyes wide with wonder. "I don't?"

"Nope. You look like a very mature young lady." He stood, offering her his hand. "How about you being my dinner companion for the evening?"

Staring up at him, she slipped her hand in his. "Really?" Keeping her face turned up, her eyes fixed on him as if at any moment he might disappear, she guided him toward the backyard, pushing the baby carriage ahead of her.

A cloud of black, throat-clogging smoke greeted them as they turned the corner at the back of the house. CeeCee stopped at the edge of the brick patio and smiled sweetly up at Rand. "I hope you like your hamburgers burnt. That's how Mama makes them best."

It took Rand a good five minutes to fight his way through the smoke and find the grill. He flipped open the lid, then jumped back when orange-yellow flames leapt up at him, singeing the hairs on his arms. Grabbing a spatula, he shoveled charred meat from the grill to the platter sitting on the grill's redwood tray.

"Are they done?"

Rand glanced up to see a smiling Cecile jogging across the lawn toward him. Frowning, he held up a blackened patty for her inspection. "Depends on how you like them cooked." He tossed the disgusting chunk of meat on the platter. "Do you have any more meat?"

Cecile stopped at his side, her hands on her hips as she studied the platter. "Sure, but why? Don't you think there'll be enough for everyone?"

Rand stared at the back of her head, hoping she was teasing. Something told him she wasn't. "No, I think there's more than enough. I was just worried about the kids chipping a tooth or bloodying a lip when they bite into one of these."

Cecile cocked her head to shoot him a grin. "Don't tell me, Dr. Coursey. Besides being blessed with a charming personality, you can cook, too?"

Rand deepened his frown, but found he couldn't—as badly as he'd wanted to—be angered by the sarcastic remark. She looked so damn cute, standing there in cutoffs and a tank top, fresh from a roll on the lawn with her children, impishly grinning up at him. In spite of himself, he grinned back.

"Yes, but I can't sew worth a dime. Pity, isn't it?"

Dusk had given way to night when Rand found himself enthroned on the patio in a glider with Cecile beside him. CeeCee had given up the ghost more than an hour before and was fast asleep in her room. Earlier, Joey's mother had called just to make sure her son was with the Kingsleys and to ensure he had a ride home. Somehow Cecile had persuaded the woman to allow the boy to stay overnight. Now all three boys—Dent, Gordy and Joey—were chin-deep on the den floor, watching a sci-fi movie on cable.

At Rand's feet June bugs performed their own version of break dancing on the brick patio while fireflies and other insects turned into kamikaze pilots and dive-bombed the citronella candles Cecile had left burning on the table.

Cecile gently pushed a bare toe against the brick patio and set the glider in motion. She lifted her face to a star-studded sky and dropped her head back against the cushion with a sigh. Rand found it impossible not to stare. The tomboy was gone and in her place, a soft and seductive woman.

After participating in a watermelon seed-spitting contest with her children, she'd changed from her sticky cutoffs and tank top into a voluminous white cotton dress with about a nine-inch ruffle whose hem hit her mid-calf. Bathed in moonlight, she appeared ethereal, angelic. Usually shaded more gold than blond, her hair glowed almost silver in the light of the moon. A gentle breeze lifted a tendril from her neck and feathered it across her face. Unable to resist, Rand lifted the hair and tucked it behind her ear.

"You're very good with them, you know."

Lazily, Cecile rolled her head to look at him. "Good with who?"

Charmed that she'd even have to ask, he smiled. "The kids. They adore you."

"Oh, them," she said as she brushed the compliment aside. Chuckling, she tipped back her head to stare at the sky. "Mother says its because I act just like them." She sighed, her expression growing wistful. "In a way, I guess I do. For years they were my buddies. I looked to them for entertainment, companionship and love. They've never once let me down."

In her explanation, Rand heard what she didn't say: that her husband, who should have provided all those things for her, *had* let her down.

"Will you ever forgive him?"

Cecile frowned, irritated that he'd read more into what she'd said than she intended to reveal. "I forgave him. The day I buried him." She twisted her head to look at Rand, her eyes emotionless. "Any other questions, Dr. Coursey?"

"Sorry. I didn't mean to pry."

"No. I'm sure you didn't." Sighing, she turned her attention once again to the sky, resolved not to argue with him since he'd done her a tremendous favor in bringing Joey to her home. "Joey seemed to be okay."

"Yes. Nothing seemed to be amiss at the house. Although, in my opinion, his mother is a little negligent in leaving a boy his age alone and to his own devices. I tried to check him over without being too obvious. I didn't see any marks or bruises."

"I didn't, either." Cecile caught the corner of her lip between her teeth and bit it. "But I still think there's something fishy going on. I've seen the bruises and I've met the boyfriend. He has arms like Popeye and a personality like a caged lion."

The hamburger Rand had eaten a few hours earlier rolled in his stomach. He knew what kind of damage "arms like Popeye" could do to a small boy. "We'll both keep an eye on him."

They rocked on for a time, each absorbed in their own thoughts before Rand remembered his offer to the boy. "Joey said he wasn't at practice because he didn't have a ride. I told him if that happened in the future, he could call me and I'd pick him up."

Cecile looked at him in surprise. "Rand! How sweet."

He shrugged, embarrassed. "It's not that far out of my way. Besides, it'll give me an opportunity to monitor the situation."

Cecile placed a hand on his thigh and squeezed, smiling her gratitude. "Just the same, I think you're sweet." She shuddered, then cut her gaze to his. "I can't believe I said that."

"What? That I'm sweet?"

"Yeah," she said, moving her hands to curl them around the seat of the swing while lifting her feet to admire her toenail polish. "Imagine that. Me, Cecile Kingsley, saying a doctor is sweet. Wonders never cease."

Though the bubble of laughter was there in her voice, Rand suspected there was more truth in the statement than Cecile would like to admit.

Taking a chance, he draped an arm along the swing's back, his fingertips brushing the top of her bare arm. "Believe it or not, there are a few of us out there."

Cecile winced as she lowered her feet to push at the bricks, setting the glider into motion again. "I guess I've been pretty rough on you, huh?"

"If you consider the number of daggers I've pulled from my skin, yes, I'd say you were pretty rough."

She shrugged her shoulders to her ears and let them drop. "Sorry. It's nothing personal, just a form of self-preservation I developed over the years."

"Do you think we could be friends, then?"

Cecile cocked her head his way and gave him a long, measuring look. "I suppose," she finally said. "In fact, your timing couldn't be any better, Dr. Coursey." Her eyes sparked mischievously. "You see, it seems I have one slot open on my friend list. I was considering letting our friend Popeye have it. But—" she shrugged, a grin chipping at her mouth "—what the heck. You asked first."

Five

Rand tossed back his head and laughed, hugging Cecile to his side. "Thanks . . . I think."

Pressed against him, it was only natural for Cecile's hand to drift to his chest and her head to his shoulder. As a result, she heard and felt his laughter rumble through his chest. She also felt muscle—lean, hard pads of muscle. Her curiosity already aroused by his physique, the strength of his embrace made her tip her head up to stare at him.

"Can I ask you a question?"

"Yes."

"Even if it's personal and sort of nosy?"

"Well, I suppose that would depend on how personal and just how nosy."

"How do you stay in shape? I mean, forgive me for saying so, but you don't seem at all like the athletic type."

Rand chuckled at her bluntness. "Swimming."

Her mouth puckered into a pout. "I should have guessed."

"Why?"

"Your shoulders, your arms, your thighs... you're built like a swimmer."

Rand laughed again, his eyes teasing. "And what do you know about my shoulders, arms and thighs?"

Cecile frowned at him, unwillingly to admit to him she'd first noticed these attributes the morning she'd awakened with him in her bed. "I'm not blind."

"Or shy, either."

"No, much to my mother's dismay." She twisted around to flatten her hands on his chest. Without any sign of inhibition, she skimmed her hands up his chest and along the breadth of his shoulders, then in a downward slide to measure his biceps. Though her touch was clinical at best, Rand felt his blood heat in response.

"At least an hour a day," she murmured to herself.

Rand tucked his chin and arched a brow at her. "How did you know that?"

"To maintain that kind of muscle tone takes work, and I figure swimming would require an hour a day. Am I right?"

"Amazingly, yes."

"Want to challenge me?"

He shook his head to clear it. He was having a hard time keeping up with the conversation—especially since his attention was centered on the dimples he'd just discovered when she'd made the offer. "What?"

"To a race. The length of the pool and back."

Rand quirked his mouth in a rueful smile. "Though the idea sounds inviting, I don't have a suit."

Cecile bounded from the glider. "No problem. There are a couple of spares in the cabana by the pool. Help yourself while I check on the boys and change."

* * *

Rand sat on the edge of the pool, slowly dragging his feet through the cool, moonlit water. A towel draped his lap and he wasn't at all sure he'd find the courage to remove it when Cecile reappeared. The only trunks he'd found in the cabana were bikini-style and made out of a skimpy strip of leopard-skin fabric. He felt like Tarzan, or worse a fool.

He couldn't help wondering who the trunks belonged to. Denton Kingsley, her ex-husband? Or maybe one of her lovers?

The thought of wearing Denton's suit was distasteful to Rand, but the thought of wearing one of Cecile's boyfriend's suits repulsed him more. The emotion didn't surprise him for he'd already discovered he was beginning to feel a little possessive where she was concerned.

"The boys are all asleep."

The sound of her voice wafted to him through the shadows of the border of trees separating the pool from the house. Rand glanced up and watched as she stepped out of the shadows, ghostlike, still wearing the long white dress.

"Did you find some trunks?"

He gathered the towel more closely to his lap, staring at her, feeling naked in comparison. "Yeah. If you can call them trunks."

Cecile hitched her dress to the top of her thighs, gained a new handhold of the voluminous fabric and flung it up and over her head. She shook her hair free while the dress drifted away behind her like a cloud chased by the wind. Without realizing he'd even been holding it, Rand released a pent-up breath. Expecting a string bikini, he was knocked senseless when he discovered Cecile wore a black maillot, seductive and evocative in its simplicity.

Graceful as a cat, she moved to the edge of the pool.

"Well? Are you ready?" she asked, peering down at him.

"Uh, yeah, I guess." Rand stood, still clutching the towel at his waist.

Cecile bit back a smile, knowing, without even seeing them, which trunks Rand had found to wear. She touched the tip of her finger to the corner of her mouth, thoughtfully. "I think there was a song back in the 50s which might be appropriate right now. Something about an itsy, bitsy, teeny, weeny bikini."

Rand tightened his fingers on the towel as heat creeped up his neck. "It was the only one I could find."

Cecile stepped back, then walked around him, giving him the once-over. Catching him off guard, she yanked the towel from his waist. Her eyes widened appreciatively. "Well, well, well, Dr. Coursey," she said as she circled him again. "I must say you fill them out better than Tony."

"Tony?"

"My brother, the cop. Remember? The one who gave me the billy club."

Rand felt an immense relief knowing the trunks belonged to her brother. "Yeah, right. The cop."

"Nice buns." Cecile gave him a pat on the behind as she moved to the edge of the pool. She cocked her head to look back at him, smiling impishly. "Ready?"

Without knowing why, Rand suddenly felt in over his head. He'd grown accustomed to and accepted the arm's length relationship Cecile had demanded from their first meeting. Now she'd done an abrupt about-face—teasing him, patting him on the butt, leering at him as if he were a male stripper placed on earth for her sole entertainment.

He'd thought her cold, even frigid. Instead, he was having to come to terms with this bold, sexual free spirit he was now confronted with—and was having a hard time doing so.

Filling his lungs with a much-needed breath, he moved to stand beside her. "As ready as I'll ever be."

"On your mark ... get set ... Go!" Cecile dived into the pool, with Rand cutting through the water a split second behind her. He quickly caught her and matched his strokes to hers, measuring her strength and endurance. A competent swimmer, he wasn't anxious to be out-stroked by a woman. Especially Cecile. He had a feeling if she beat him, she'd never let him live down the defeat.

Keeping a careful eye on her as they approached the opposite side of the pool, he neatly flipped and pushed off, shooting a good length ahead of her. About halfway to the finish line, it suddenly occurred to him that beating her might be as bad as losing to Cecile. She struck him as the competitive type, never satisfied until she'd evened the score. If he beat her, she might very well demand a rematch. Rand couldn't decide which would be worse: an angry Cecile because she'd lost the race, or a gloating Cecile because she'd won. He found neither scenario appealing.

Troubled over this complexity, Rand slowed his strokes, trying to think of a way out of the predicament. Inspiration struck just short of the finish line. Ducking beneath the water, he quickly kicked to the bottom and watched for Cecile's form to appear above him. As soon as he spotted her, he pushed off, angling his body so that he rose directly beneath her. Catching her around the waist, he pulled her under.

Her arms flailing, she faced him, her cheeks puffed, her lips puckered. She looked like a bug-eyed fish—a beautiful, if indignant, bug-eyed fish. The temptation was simply too great. Pulling her closer, he pressed his lips to hers.

Water pulsed around them in a world robbed of sound. There was only touch and taste, and Rand couldn't get enough of either. His hands left her waist to roam her back while his mouth sought continuously new angles against the fullness of her lips.

Frustrated, his lungs burning, he kicked to the surface, bringing Cecile with him. They broke through the water simultaneously, each gasping, water running down their faces, their eyes riveted on each other.

They were both surprised, but it was Cecile who spoke first. "Do that again," she gasped.

"Do what?"

"Kiss me."

More than willing to oblige, he took her mouth in a deep, searching kiss, drawing her with him as he sought shallower water. When his toes scraped bottom, he stood, bracing himself as he pulled Cecile flush against him, never once releasing his hold on her.

As he slowly withdrew his lips, Cecile closed her eyes and dropped back her head. "Oh, God," she murmured in a pained voice, her fingernails digging into his shoulders.

"Is something wrong?" he asked in concern.

"I was sure it was my imagination."

"What was?"

"My reaction to you." She lowered her chin until her eyes met his. Passion heated her blue eyes, turning them smoky. "When I woke up with you in my bed the other morning, I told myself that it had to be the result of a dream or my semi-conscious state, that there was no way in hell you could draw such a response from me."

"And?"

"I was wrong."

A grin chipped at the corner of his mouth. "How wrong?"

"Dead wrong," she whispered, her eyes drifting closed as she leaned into him, anxious to find his lips once again. She framed his face with her hands, seeking the utmost pleasures of his mouth as she pressed her body flush against his. The swell of thigh muscles, pumped from the exertion of swimming, pressed hard against hers, driving her pelvis firmly against his groin. The sensation was not one she was anxious to escape.

The thrust and rasp of spandex-covered breasts against his chest both intrigued and frustrated Rand. Cupping Cecile's hips in his hands, he lifted her, guiding her legs around his waist. Her femininity sucked at him like a magnet, nearly driving him mad with the need to rip off the scraps of material separating them and fill her with a hardness that had already started to ache.

Tearing her lips from his, Cecile clung to his shoulders as she dropped her head back. She locked her legs tight around him, savoring the heat and tautness of his abdomen against that most feminine part of her that pulsed with her need for him.

Groaning at the sensuous pressure, Rand pressed his lips to her bared throat, then scraped them down in a sultry trail, heating her chilled skin until his chin bumped the elastic top of her suit. Moving his hands to her shoulders, he caught the suit's thin straps in his fingers and dragged them down her arms, baring her breasts.

Pebbled from the cold water and fully aroused, her breasts bobbed pearlescent in the moonlit water just out of reach. "Dear God, Cecile," he whispered almost reverently.

Gathering his head between her hands, Cecile guided his face to her, arching her back, moaning her pleasure when his lips found a budded nipple. Sensations, hot and demanding, ripped through her as he greedily nipped and suckled, leaving her moist and wanting.

Responding to the increased tempo of her hips rubbing against his groin, Rand slid his hands down her back and gently kneaded the cheeks of her buttocks. Slipping a finger beneath the suit's elastic band, he gently skimmed his hands down and around, molding her cheeks within his palms as he sought her feminine core. Hot and moist, her velvety skin throbbed, silently crying out for his touch.

Wetting his finger in the honeyed moistness, he traced his fingers in a circular path, keeping his touch gentle, his rhythm achingly slow, until she writhed beneath him. When he felt she could stand no more, he slipped his finger within and felt the tightening of her muscles around him.

"Oh, Rand," she cried, tensing.

"It's okay," he whispered, soothing her with his voice as well his hands. "Just relax."

"But—"

"No buts. Just enjoy."

"Oh, Rand," she moaned weakly, arching away from him. The movement thrust her hips hard against him and a breast just within his reach. Rand took the tempting orb between his teeth, drawing it deep into his mouth and emulating the rhythm of his finger moving within her.

"Rand!" she cried breathlessly. "Oh, Rand, please—" Before she could finish her request, her body stiffened and he held her against him while the pulsations of her climax throbbed around him.

After a long moment she dropped her forehead to his shoulder, her chest heaving, her body growing lax. "I'm sorry," she gasped. "I should've—"

"No." He pressed his lips to her hair. "You've absolutely nothing to be sorry about."

He let his finger slide from her and wrapped his arms around her, holding her near. Closing his eyes, he buried his face in the tangled wetness of her hair and let the cool, soothing water of the pool work at the ache she'd left him with.

Rand awakened with a jerk, drenched in sweat, his body trembling and the sheets twisted around the lower half of his body. Lying still, his heart thudding against his rib cage, he stared at the shadowed ceiling, trying to remember what had awakened him.

The dream.

He groaned, squeezing his fists against his eyes, trying to block the memory, but failed. Tears burned behind his eyelids and anguish tightened his chest as the vision of the little boy from his dream formed.

Standing on the side of the street, his arms outstretched, hot, desperate tears streaking his face, the child screamed until his face grew red and hiccups distorted his pleas. But the car he watched, the one carrying his mother farther and farther away from him, continued down the street, as if impervious to his misery.

A woman appeared beside the boy, her voice gentle and soothing, and reached for his hand, but the child jerked away. He ran down the street, chasing the car, screaming for it to stop. Blinded by tears, he stumbled and fell, the pavement chewing at the bare skin on his face, knees and elbows. He lifted his head, blood blending with the tears streaking down his cheeks, and watched the car disappear from sight.

A shudder racked Rand's body from head to toe as the vision drifted away. He hadn't dreamed that dream in years. Why had it surfaced now?

He plowed his forehead into deep furrows, trying hard to think of an explanation, but instead of a solution, a second part of the dream surfaced, something he'd never dreamed before.

In the vision, a man stood on one side of a gaping cavern, a woman on the other, each reaching out for the other. The man strained, putting all his strength into the effort to help her across to his side. Just as their fingers touched, a child's voice called and the woman glanced behind her at a huddle of solemn-faced children. While her face was turned away, the gap suddenly widened, slowly peeling away his tenacious hold on her. Like a ravenous animal, the dark gap hungrily engulfed her and left him holding nothing but air.

Rand swallowed hard, wiping a hand at the perspiration beading his upper lip. He didn't need an analyst to interpret the dream for him. He understood the meaning all too well. It was an omen, a warning for him to heed.

A relationship with Cecile Kingsley would bring him as much heartbreak as that which he had suffered as a child. And because he understood the emotions suffered by the solemn-faced children in the dream, he knew he'd never make Cecile choose between her children and him.

Blended families seldom made happy families. Rand Coursey was living proof.

Cecile glanced up just in time to see Rand drive up. If asked why her heartbeat accelerated and her hands grew clumsy at the sight, she'd have sworn the effects were due to her relief to see that Joey was in the passenger seat beside him. But she was an honest woman—if only to herself—and admitted the sight of Rand was the real cause.

She watched him make his way through the tangle of parents knotting the sidewalk, strolling along beside Joey, his hand resting on the boy's shoulder. Dressed in black athletic shorts and a crisp, white golf shirt, he looked handsome, endearing and totally masculine.

Not even trying to hide her pleasure, Cecile stood poised at the gate to the dugout smiling a welcome, her hands hidden behind her back.

"Rand Coursey, you look like a real coach," she said proudly.

He glanced up, his look growing wary. "I do?"

"Well, almost." Her smile melted into a frown as she circled him, giving him the once-over. "But you'd look better if you'd wear this."

She whipped a T-shirt from behind her and held it up for him to see White Sox lettered in white across the T-shirt's black front. She reversed it, displaying the word Coach in bold white print. She dipped her head over the shirt to read the print with him. "The boys wanted you to have one, so they all chipped in and bought it for you."

Rand felt a knot of emotion rise in his throat. The boys had done this for him, which was a sign that they had accepted him as their coach. He reached out and took the shirt. "I'm honored." Feeling awkward and not knowing what else to say, he asked, "Are they all here?"

"Yep. Running laps. Joey," she said, turning her attention to the boy who stood behind Rand. "You'll be the lead-off pitcher, so why don't you hit the mound and warm up with the catcher?"

Joey took off, leaving Cecile and Rand alone in the dugout. Rand watched him jog to the pitcher's mound.

Cecile saw the tension around his eyes and feared something had happened to Joey. "Is he okay?" she asked.

Rand glanced her way. "Yeah. I think. He seems a bit keyed-up, though."

Cecile smiled and moved to pat him on the back. "So do you."

Rand stepped from her touch and started organizing equipment. "First game jitters."

Assuming his uneasiness was in fact due to a bad case of nerves, she tried to reassure him. "You'll do fine. As third base coach, you just need to remember who's running the bases. Some of the guys are faster than others and are more likely to steal successfully. Others, like Brandt, you'll need to hold back. He's a good hitter, but slow as Christmas.

Unless you're sure he can make it, signal him to stay on base. Got it?"

Rand let out a tense breath. "Yeah, I hope."

"Relax and put on your shirt, Coach."

Rand glanced her way, his frown deepening. "Now?"

"Yes, now, silly. The boys will be disappointed if you don't wear it, and the game's about to start."

When he didn't move, Cecile said, "Well?"

The thought of stripping in front of Cecile spoke of a familiarity and intimacy Rand had already decided was pointless. Stalling for time, hoping she'd leave the dugout, he halfheartedly tugged his shirttail from the waistband of his shorts.

"Oh, for heaven's sake," Cecile exclaimed in exasperation. "You'd think I've never seen you bare-chested before." Quickly crossing to him, she caught the bottom of his shirt and yanked upward, ripping the shirt over his head.

When she scooped the new T-shirt from the bench and turned to him, obviously intending to dress him, Rand snatched the shirt away from her. "I can dress myself, thank you," he said irritably.

She stared at him a full minute before pursing her lips. "Okay, Coursey. What's the deal?"

"Nothing." He tugged the shirt over his head. "I just don't care for public displays of nudity."

"I hardly think a bare chest registers as public nudity, so let's hear it. What's bugging you?"

Rand sank to the bench, avoiding her gaze as he slowly tucked the shirt beneath his short's waistband.

"It's about last night, isn't it?" she said, narrowing an eye at him. "Are you worried you came on too strong, or are you hacked because all the pleasure was mine?"

"Oh, for God's sake," he exclaimed as he leapt to his feet, intent on escaping the dugout and Cecile's blunt inquiry.

She planted a hand on his chest and pushed him right back down onto the bench.

Not wanting to create a scene, Rand remained there, scowling up at her. "Okay, if you insist. Yes, it's about last night," he said, his voice tight with irritation. "And, no, I'm not worried I came on too strong." He glanced around to make sure no one was within hearing distance. "And I'm not hacked because all the pleasure was yours. For your information, I rather enjoyed myself, too."

Cecile tossed up her hands. "Then what's the problem?"

Unlike Cecile, Rand didn't particularly want to address this issue, especially not now. He dropped his forearms to his knees, laced his fingers together and stared at the dirt between his spread feet, trying to figure out what and how much to say. He wanted her to know his feelings, but didn't want to offend her. "I just don't think it would be wise for us to get involved."

"Why?"

Frustrated that she wouldn't drop the subject, Rand heaved a slow breath. "You're a nice woman, Cecile, but I'm just not prepared to take on a family."

Her eyes grew wide. "A family!" she echoed back at him. "Who the heck asked you to take on my family? Of all the unmitigated gall—" She dropped her arms to her sides and swung away from him, muttering curses under her breath, then whipped back, leveling a finger at his nose. "For your information, Dr. Coursey, I'm not looking for a husband. A lover, yes, I'd consider you for that position. But a husband? No thanks!"

* * *

Rand knew it was foolish, for he was the one who had wanted to terminate his relationship with Cecile before anyone was hurt, but her saying she wouldn't have him for a husband—well, that rankled more than he'd like to admit.

From the third base line he watched her, standing at first, her hair tucked beneath a baseball cap. Her hands were on her hips, and her eyes riveted on the pitcher, watching for an opportunity to send the runner at first to second on a steal. That she could keep her mind on the game really ticked Rand off, for he couldn't think of anything but the fact that she had rejected him as a potential husband.

As if she were any prize, he thought spitefully. He stared hard at her, looking for faults to justify his newfound stance.

She dresses like a boy half the time, he decided, and cusses like a sailor. She's temperamental, stubborn, opinionated and . . . His thoughts scattered like leaves in the wind as she lifted her arms above her head and went through a series of complicated hand signals to tell the batter to bunt.

The movement pulled her T-shirt tight across her breasts, emphasizing their ripe, full shape. Thankfully, tonight she'd chosen to wear a bra. But the added barrier couldn't shield Rand from drawing a memory of the texture and fullness of her breasts. Or the sweetness of their taste.

"Oh, hell," he mumbled under his breath as he turned away, disgusted by his own hormones.

A cracking sound and a roar from the crowd had him turning back. Brandt was running hard for first, with Cecile frantically waving him on. Joey was poised at second, looking expectantly at Rand. Remembering his duties as third base coach, Rand waved for Joey to run. While Joey peeled out, dirt flying from beneath his cleats, Rand checked for the position of the ball and watched it sail over the right fielder's head.

Jumping up and down, Rand waved Joey past third and sent him for home. With Brandt rounding second, Rand felt a moment of panic. He shifted his gaze to the scoreboard. The score was 6-5 in the bottom of the seventh. Could the kid make it? If he did, with Joey's tying run, the White Sox would win, and Brandt would be a hero instead of the team's worst player.

But Cecile had already warned him the kid was as slow as Christmas. He glanced again at right field and saw the player scoop the ball from the grass.

He cut his gaze to Cecile, who was looking at him, signaling him to hold Brandt at third. From the corner of his eye, Rand saw the ball leave the right fielder's hand. Brandt was a step away from third.

In a split second, Rand made the decision.

As Brandt's foot hit third base, Rand yelled, "Go for it, kid, you can do it!" He closed his eyes and lifted his face to heaven, praying Brandt would make it—but not before he saw the look of horror on Cecile's face.

The kid could do it. Rand knew he could. Unable to stand the suspense, he opened his eyes in time to see Brandt drop to a hip and slide. The ball hit the catcher's mitt and red dust churned like a whirlwind around home plate.

"Safe!" yelled the man in blue. "That's the game."

His heart hammering against his chest and his face split with a proud smile, Rand raced down the third base line. He hauled Brandt to his feet and hoisted him to his shoulder. The rest of the team flooded out of the dugout and quickly surrounded them, cheering and yelling. Beaming, Rand turned to see Cecile marching toward them.

"Nice call," she muttered as she stormed past him for the dugout.

Rand lowered Brandt to the ground, gave him a pat on the back and guided the boys to form the traditional line to shake hands with the players of the losing team.

The field and stands were empty, and the boys were running for the concession stand for their victory drink when Rand headed for the dugout. Cecile was inside, angrily stuffing bats and balls into the equipment bag.

"You shouldn't have sent him home," she muttered as he walked past her.

Still pumped up by the victory, Rand replied offhandedly, "Probably not, but he made it."

"What if he'd been thrown out at home?"

"Then the score would have been tied and we would have gone into overtime."

Cecile rolled her eyes. "I don't care about the game. What about Brandt? If he'd been thrown out, he'd have felt lousy."

"But he didn't get thrown out and now he's a hero." He took the bag from her hand, cinched up the opening and tossed it over his shoulder. Feeling more reckless than he had in years, he shot her a cocky grin. "You've got to learn to take chances, Cecile. Otherwise, life's boring."

He trudged past her, but stopped and turned back after only three steps. "Oh, and by the way," he said, still grinning. "I accept your offer as lover." Touching his index finger to the brim of his baseball cap, he turned, whistling a cheery little tune as he headed for the concession stands to bask in the glow of victory with his players.

Six

Cecile dropped her hand from the key she'd just pushed into the back door of her house. With her boys camping out in the Brannan's backyard and CeeCee at her mother's for an overnight visit, she found the prospect of entering the dark house uninviting. Lonely, and not in the least bit sleepy, she dragged out the key. She scuffed across the patio and down the moonlit brick path to the pool.

Flopping down in a lounge chair, she propped her elbow on the chair arm and her cheek on her palm. A light breeze cooled her cheeks and attempted to tease her into taking a dip in the pool by wafting the scent of chlorine beneath her nose. But Cecile would have none of that.

"Rand Coursey is a jerk," she muttered, glaring at the water lapping at the pool edge. "An unmitigated, egocentric, ass of a jerk!"

I accept your offer as lover. The nerve of the guy! As if she wanted or needed him as a lover, anyway. Her fingers tapped out a fast staccato beat against the chair's armrest while she continued to glare at the water.

Granted, at the moment, she didn't have a man in her life. But that was Josh's fault—Josh Wagner, the last in a long list of men who'd sought her company after Denton's death.

Six months into their relationship, he'd started acting like a husband, making demands on her time, always jealous of anything that diverted her attention from him, expecting her to wait on him hand and foot. The fact that he treated her kids just a hair less than human beings drove the final nail in their relationship's coffin.

Not that she missed Josh, she thought petulantly. She didn't. In her estimation, the relationship had lasted about two months longer than it should have. Though they'd shared much in common, it hadn't taken long to discover his muscles outweighed his brain matter ten to one.

And he'd been a selfish lover, she remembered, concerned with his own pleasure without much thought to hers. Not at all like Rand.

The thought of Rand had her emitting a low growl. She shoved from the chair to pace the edge of the pool. As always, action calmed her and helped her think—but certainly didn't remove Rand Coursey from her thoughts.

Okay, she admitted grudgingly after several minutes of pacing, so Rand had shown himself to be a considerate lover. And yes, she further conceded, he was capable of carrying on an intelligent conversation, and he was kind to the point of aggravation.

And that kindness extended to kids. She stopped at the edge of the pool to stare at her blurred reflection in the water. A reluctant smile tipped one corner of her mouth as she envisioned him charging down the third base line, his hands chopping the air above his head like helicopter blades before he'd hauled Brandt to his shoulder. Judging by the exuberant expression on the kid's face, that home run might well be the turning point in the boy's baseball career. Thanks to Rand's willingness to take a chance on him, Brandt had proven himself worthy to his teammates.

Sighing, Cecile sat down, dragged off her shoes and socks and dipped her feet, toes first, into the pool. The night was hot and muggy, and when the cold water hit her warm skin, a slight shiver shook her. Water lapped at her legs, its gentle ebb and flow a sensual massage. She closed her eyes and tipped back her head, enjoying the sensation.

Memories of Rand's hands moving over her in much the same way as the water had goose bumps popping out on her arms, making her shudder deliciously. His touch had been gentle, soothing...yet, oh, so erotic.

Her nipples tightened as she remembered the feel of his mouth suckling at them and the feel of his hands roaming over her skin, heating her body to fever pitch. He was a gifted lover, knowing just the right places to touch and the exact amount of pressure to apply to have her all but begging for more.

Cecile flipped open her eyes, shocked to discover her breath had shortened until she was almost panting. Appalled by her body's reaction to a simple memory, she scrambled to her feet, water dripping down her legs.

"The cad," she cried. "How does he do this to me?"

Sleepily, Rand pulled open the door, only to have a palm shoved against his chest. He stumbled back, as Cecile stormed past him.

"There are a few details we need to discuss," she said, slamming the door behind her. "Where's your bedroom?"

"W-what?"

"Your bedroom. You know, the place where you sleep."

More asleep than awake, Rand lifted an arm and pointed down the hall to his left. Cecile wheeled and headed that way. Not sure what she was up to, he followed.

Once inside his room, she dropped her shoes and socks to the floor. "First off, I'm not looking for a husband, so you can get that notion out of your head right now." She caught the hem of her T-shirt and ripped it over her head. "Secondly," she said as she tossed the T-shirt to join her shoes on the floor, "I don't need your money. Thanks to Denton, I've got a buttload of it myself." She added her bra to the heap, then caught the waist of her shorts in the curve of her thumbs and shoved them and a pair of black bikini panties to her ankles.

Without a shred of modesty, she stepped out of her clothes, strolled to the bed and flipped back the covers. "Thirdly, our relationship will remain strictly physical." She tested the firmness of the mattress with the tips of her fingers. "Well," she amended after a moment's thought. "Maybe not totally physical. We will be sharing godparent responsibilities of the Brannan children and coaching responsibilities of the team. But as far as you and I are concerned, this is a physical relationship, nothing more. I don't expect or want to be romanced by you, and if the word 'love' ever passes your lips, I'm history."

Satisfied with both the bed and her list of contingencies, she twisted around to look at Rand over her shoulder. "Agreed?"

Rand could barely breathe, much less speak. Cecile was dynamite in a bathing suit, but naked, she was devastating. Angled as she was, a budded nipple peeked from behind the shield of her arm, tempting him with the remembrance of her breasts' silken texture and delectable taste. Below her elbow, tanned skin stretched over a taut, flat abdomen before sloping down to span a swell of pelvic bone. The cheeks of her butt were fully visible. They were firm and rounded, as he remembered them to be, and sized just right to fill a man's hands.

A cautious person, Rand didn't dare allow himself to cross to her until he was sure what he was getting himself in to. "A strictly physical relationship," he repeated slowly.

Cecile flopped down on the bed. "Yep."

"No strings attached from either party."

"Exactly. So what do you say?" She lifted her face, her gaze challenging.

It was a hardship, especially with her sprawled naked and inviting on his bed, but Rand held up a hand. To stop himself or her, he wasn't sure which. "Just one thing."

"What?"

"If either one of us decides to terminate the physical aspects of our relationship, the other party must agree to end it on friendly terms, no feelings hurt."

Cecile shrugged nonchalantly. "Suits me."

Rand let out a slow, ragged breath. With the deal now cut, he wasn't sure what to do next. For some reason, it all seemed so cold-blooded and calculated.

"Would you like a glass of wine?" he asked.

Cecile pursed her lips to hide a smile. She hadn't expected shyness, but decided on Rand, anything else would have been totally out of character. "That would be nice."

He left and returned shortly bearing a bamboo tray loaded with a bottle of wine, two fluted glasses and a platter heaped with cheese, crackers and fruit. He set it on the bedside table, but Cecile quickly transferred it to the center of the bed. She patted the spot next to her as she crawled on her knees to snag a cluster of grapes from the platter. She popped one in her mouth, then plucked another, angling her body to offer the fruit to Rand as he eased down onto the bed beside her.

When he lifted his hand, she nudged it aside and grinned as she scooted closer to place the grape directly into his mouth. He caught it between his teeth, then closed his lips over it, slowly drawing it into his mouth, his gaze riveted on her.

"Good, aren't they?" Her voice was low and husky and surprisingly calm, which added to Rand's increasing discomfort.

"Yes, they are." Not sure what was expected of him, he reached for the bottle of wine, silently damning the slight tremble of his hand. When the cork broke free, a muffled pop broke the awkward silence in the room. He tipped the bottle over one glass, then the other, filling each half full with a sparkling Chardonnay, while Cecile watched his every movement.

She leaned toward him, her breasts brushing his arm as she reached for a glass. Settling back against the pillows, she lifted her glass in a toast. "Here's mud in your eye, Coursey." A droplet of wine dripped from her glass and hit her high on the chest, then rolled down the slope of her breast and hung precariously on the very tip of her nipple.

"Yeah," he whispered, his gaze locked on the droplet of wine. "Whatever." Lifting the tray, he sat it on the floor, then crawled across the bed. He braced a hand on either side of her hips, then lowered his head over her breast. His tongue snaked out and licked at the single droplet of wine suspended there.

The rasp of his tongue against her nipple had Cecile curling her fingers around the wineglass she clasped above his head. Closing her eyes, she smiled and slid farther down into the pillows, giving him easier access. "I love the way you do that," she whispered.

"Do you?"

In answer, she dipped a finger in her glass and smeared wine over the opposite nipple. Thirstily, Rand lapped it away, then drew the budded orb into his mouth. His tongue teased while his mouth suckled. An ache throbbed to life between Cecile's legs.

Placing her glass on the bedside table, she spread her legs and guided Rand until the bulk of his body lay between them. The added weight and warmth snugged tight against her created a swirl of sensation within. With a sigh of contentment, she buried her fingers in his hair, knowing that of all the impulsive decisions she'd made in her life, this one had to be the best.

"Rand?"

His muffled "hmm" reverberated against Cecile's bare abdomen, making her chuckle.

"Did Jack call you today?"

He lifted his head a fraction of an inch. "About the twins' christening?"

"Yeah."

He lowered his head, nuzzling his cheek against the warmth of her stomach. "I vaguely remember him mentioning something about that. When is it?"

"Sunday, you jerk," she said, ruffling his hair. "Nine o'clock sharp. And you better be there." Her fingers gentled as she massaged his scalp from the crown of his head to the base of his neck, deep in thought. "I'm considering having a brunch afterward at my house. What do you think?"

"Are you planning on having it catered?"

Puzzled, Cecile frowned at the back of his head. "No. I was thinking of something more personal and private. Just the family." Warming to the idea, she resumed the movement of her fingers in his hair. "I borrowed some recipes from my mother. I thought we'd have a sausage and spin-ach quiche, miniature blueberry muffins and cheese grits. I found a darling picture in a magazine of a baby's cradle carved from a watermelon shell and filled with fresh fruit, which would look terrific as a centerpiece.''

When he didn't respond, she caught his hair in her hands and lifted until she could see his face. "You don't sound too enthusiastic."

Enthusiastic? No, he wasn't. The memory of the charred hamburgers was too fresh in his mind and on his palette for Rand to be enthusiastic about any culinary offerings from Cecile. But as he looked into her eyes, still shaded a smoky blue as a result of their lovemaking, he chose not to offend her. He tried for diplomacy instead. "Do you think you'd have time? I mean, you'll be at the christening, and all..." His voice drifted off feebly.

"You don't think I can do it, do you?" she asked, nar-rowing an eye at him.

Rand struggled to a sitting position. "Sure I do, honey. It's just that—"

"Save it, Coursey," she said irritably as she squirmed from beneath him. "I assure you I can pull off something as simple as a brunch for twenty."

Rand told himself it wasn't because he doubted Cecile's abilities. If she put her mind to something, he was sure she could accomplish any feat. It was simply that he felt he should help. After all, he *was* the twins' godfather. He should share in any endeavor for their benefit or in their honor. And this was a special occasion, for an infant was only christened once.

He told himself this repeatedly as he circled Cecile's block for the fourth time, trying to find the nerve to pull into her drive. He'd already noted that the kitchen light was on. He'd even seen her flit past the kitchen window once or twice. Each time he'd seen her, he'd told himself he would stop, casually walk up to the house and offer his assistance. But then, at the last moment, he would gun the engine and circle the block yet one more time, fearing that his presence would only irritate her more.

And he didn't want to anger her further. She was already ticked off at him enough.

But he couldn't let her suffer the humiliation of serving a brunch unfit for human consumption to twenty friends. Steeling himself, when he approached her drive this time, he whipped the steering wheel to the right before he could change his mind and braked his car to a stop beside the kitchen door. He sat there a moment in the quiet and safety of his car and built up his nerve. He knew it wouldn't be easy. Nothing with Cecile ever was. But he knew he had to at least offer his help.

He approached the back door burdened with a thousand misgivings. She'd resent his offer of help. She'd tell him to get out and never grace her door with his presence again. She'd scream obscenities and probably throw something at him, like a skillet, or worse, a butcher knife. Knowing Cecile, her aim would be deadly.

His feet leaden, he took the last step and lifted a fist to the door. Before his knuckles scraped wood, he heard the scream. His heart leapt to his throat. Without hesitating, he twisted open the door and bolted inside.

He saw her standing in front of the oven door, smoke billowing out around her, her hands knotted in her hair.

"Cecile?"

She wheeled, her eyes crazed, her nose dusted with flour. "Oh, Rand," she cried. Her face crumpled and she burst into tears. She whirled again and kicked the oven door closed with her foot.

Immediately, Rand was at her side, catching her in his arms, stopping her before she hurt herself. "There, there, Cecile," he soothed, gathering her close.

"You were right," she sobbed, her fingers fisting into his shirt fabric. "Everything's a mess. The quiche burned, the muffins are like rocks." She sniffed, wiping her wrist beneath her nose. "The only thing that's edible is the fruit and that's probably because I haven't started slicing it yet."

"Oh, it can't be all that bad," Rand soothed, trying to make her feel better.

"It's worse." She pulled away from him and gathered the skirt of her apron to dab at her tears. She walked to the counter and lifted a casserole for Rand's inspection.

He studied the contents and lifted a hopeful gaze to Cecile. "Fudge?"

"No." She sniffed again. "Cheese grits." She turned the casserole over and the rectangle of grits fell out, hitting the floor and making a clanking sound against the tiles before rocking to a halt, still intact.

She glanced at the clock. "It's already almost ten o'clock. There's no way in hell I can hire a caterer at this hour of the night and on such short notice. I should have listened to you."

Rand cautiously laid an arm around her shoulders. When she didn't slug him or shove him away, he found the courage to hug her reassuringly to his side. "Don't worry, Cecile. I'll help you."

She lifted her chin, her blue eyes flooded with tears. "This isn't hamburgers on the grill, Rand. This is quiche, for God's sake."

Patiently he patted her shoulder. "I know, Cecile. But I assure you that between us, we can pull this off."

He guided her to a bar stool. "You sit here, relax for a minute and dry your eyes while I mix up the pastry for the quiche."

Knowing he couldn't do a worse job of it than she already had, Cecile waved feebly toward the mess littering the top of the center island. "The recipe is there somewhere. Under the flour canister, I think."

Efficiently, Rand began reorganizing the clutter, placing the ingredients he'd require to one side. "I don't need a recipe," he said offhandedly as he moved to stack dirty dishes in the sink.

"You don't?"

"No. I've been baking since I was a kid."

Cecile curled her nose. "That's disgusting."

Rand chuckled good-naturedly. "Yes, I know. Real men don't eat quiche, much less prepare it. Right?"

"I didn't mean it offensively. It's just that I've never— even with a recipe—been able to successfully roll out a piecrust."

"I've had lots of experience." He took a clean bowl and measured flour into it. "I was a sickly kid, allergic to just about everything outside. My foster mother, Mrs. Baxter, was a proficient cook. She used to bake pies to sell for extra money." He spooned out shortening, then took a pastry cutter and cut it into the flour. "When my allergies were on the rampage and I couldn't play outside with the other kids, she'd let me help her in the kitchen." He tipped a cup of water over the mixture, tested the batter, then added a drop more. "As a result, I'm a heck of a baker."

Engrossed by his movements as much as his story, Cecile dropped her elbows to the tiled countertop and her chin to her hands, watching and listening. "I didn't know you grew up in a foster home," she said, wanting to hear more.

"From the age of ten on. That's where I met Jack. We both lived with the Baxters. Nine kids under one roof." He shuddered at the memory, then dumped the glob of batter onto a cutting board and began to knead it.

"What happened to your parents?"

Rand's hands stilled for a split second before he dipped his hand into the canister, then dusted the dough with flour. Frowning, he slapped a palm against the rounded mass to flatten it. "They were around."

"Around?"

"My mother and father divorced when I was six, and my old man took off for Wyoming. I've never heard from him since. My mother, she remarried and lives a couple of hours from here."

"If your mother was living, why did she place you in foster care?"

"Let's just say, I became a burden." He forced a smile as he glanced up and offered the rolling pin to her. "Want to roll out the dough?"

Cecile eyed the rolling pin with distaste. "If it's all the same to you, I'd rather not."

Rand chuckled, and put his muscle behind the wooden handles. "Since cooking doesn't seem to be your forte, how do you manage to nourish your children?"

Cecile arched a brow his way. "Ever heard of a microwave?"

"Aren't you going to iron it first?"

Cecile flicked the linen cloth a second time and let it settle over the tabletop. "Nope." She smoothed her hands across the fabric, flattening out what wrinkles she could.

"But it's so...so wrinkled."

Cecile stepped back, critically eyeing the cloth. "You're right," she agreed, though grudgingly. Weary and wanting nothing more than her bed, she snagged the corner of the cloth and dragged it from the table. Wadding it under her arm, she trudged toward the laundry room. "I'll just throw it in the dryer with a wet towel for a few minutes. That'll take most of the wrinkles out."

Rand caught her elbow as she passed him. "Whoa! Why not just iron it?"

"It's two o'clock in the morning, and I'm tired. Besides," she said, yawning, "I hate to iron."

She looked so pitiful, standing there in front of him, her eyelids heavy, her shoulders drooping with weariness, that Rand was tempted to gather her into his arms and carry her to bed. Instead he put his arm around her and guided her to the sofa. "Put up your feet for a minute. I'll iron."

To her credit, Cecile put up a halfhearted fight. "No, you've done enough," she argued, maintaining a tenuous hold on a corner of the cloth.

Shaking his head at her stubbornness, Rand gently pushed her to the sofa and pried her fingers from the cloth. "It won't take a minute."

"Okay, if you insist," she said on a yawn. She curled her feet under her and snuggled into the corner of the sofa. "The ironing board and iron are in the utility room. If you need anything else . . ." Her eyelashes fluttered briefly and her head drifted over to hit the sofa cushion before she ever completed the offer.

Chuckling, Rand left her there to sleep while he went in search of the utility room. Within minutes he had the iron steaming and the cloth draped over the board. Whistling under his breath, he pushed the iron across the crinkled linen.

Considering the hour and the amount of time he'd spent toiling in the kitchen, he should have been exhausted. He wasn't. In fact, he couldn't remember the last time he'd en-

joyed himself so much. Some people—like Cecile, he
thought with a chuckle—considered cooking drudgery. But
to him, puttering around the kitchen was the ultimate in re-
laxation.

Even with Cecile underfoot, talking and laughing and
generally getting in his way, he had spent four thoroughly
enjoyable hours helping her get ready for the brunch. He set
the iron on its end and readjusted the linen. The woman was
a nightmare in the kitchen and totally useless, but she was
more fun than a barrel of monkeys. She teased and laughed
and, as a result, the time had literally flown by. Unlike his
usual Saturday nights.

The thought made him pause, steam billowing from the
base of the iron to mist the hairs on his arm. The idea of
spending an evening with a woman like Cecile was as for-
eign to him as flying to the moon. On the rare occasions
when he did choose to spend a Saturday evening with a
woman, he usually chose someone much like himself.
Someone quiet and restful, who enjoyed an intellectually
stimulating conversation, a gourmet meal and a glass or two
of wine.

Not someone like Cecile, who bounded around the
kitchen like a puppy who hadn't grown into his feet, bumping into him and knocking things over, all the while laughing and teasing and patting him on the behind.

But, dang, she was fun!

"We heard a noise."

Startled, Rand glanced up to find CeeCee standing in the
doorway to the utility room, a doll hugged to her chest. She
wore a pink nightgown whose ruffled hem just brushed the
floor. Her hair was a tangled mass of curls and she was
looking at him with blue eyes darkened by fear.

"You did?"

"Yeah. I think there's a monster under my bed."

Not sure what was expected of him, Rand rounded the end of the ironing board and dropped to a knee in front of her. "What kind of monster?"

"The big, ugly and growly kind." She lifted a fist to her eye and rubbed sleepily. Rand couldn't help thinking Cecile must have looked just this way at this age.

"I bet he's gone now," he said to comfort her. "So why don't you go on back to bed."

CeeCee hitched up her nightgown and sat down on his knee, slinging an arm around his neck. "Can't."

The weight of her arm was like that of a butterfly on his neck, yet Rand had to place a hand on the floor to keep from keeling over. He couldn't remember a child ever coming to him in the middle of the night for comfort, or him feeling quite so inadequate. "Why not?"

"'Cause he never goes away until Mama comes and shoos him out from under my bed."

"Oh." He sat for a moment, trying to figure out how best to handle the situation. Groping for a solution, he explained, "Your mother's asleep on the sofa, and I really hate to wake her." When she continued to look at him, he offered, "Do you think I could shoo the monster away?"

"I don't know," she said, her forehead puckered in doubt. "But I guess you could try. But you have to be really mean, otherwise he'll come back."

"I can be pretty mean." Rand stood, catching CeeCee under the arms and hefting her up. He firmed his lips, making himself look fierce. "Now show me where this monster is."

Seven

Sunbeams bored through the stained-glass windows of the church, bathing those gathered around the altar in a heavenly glow of rose and gold. Holding Madison, Cecile stood on one side of Jack and Malinda while Rand stood on the opposite side holding Lila. Forming a protective arc behind them were the Brannan boys, looking spiffy in their Sunday best.

As far as family went, that was the sum total in the crowd of parishioners in the church, for Jack and Malinda didn't have much. The only blood kin they could claim were Malinda's parents, and, as usual, the Comptons were conspicuously absent. According to Malinda, they'd sent a card from their home in Saudi Arabia, offering their congratulations and a hefty check for the twins' college fund. How sweet, Cecile reflected without affection, but so like Malinda's parents.

Sighing, she turned her gaze to her own parents sitting on the front pew, strategically placed between Dent and Gordy. CeeCee sat perched on her grandmother's lap, her hands folded neatly, looking as sweet and cherubic as an angel.

How lucky I am, she thought, to be blessed with parents who care about their children and their grandchildren. The thought reminded her of Rand and the stories he'd told her the night before of his own childhood. That peek into his past had helped her understand him a little better. Growing up in foster homes was a heck of a way to spend your childhood, and she was sure it had left its mark. She'd known about Jack's past and knew that as an adult he'd compensated for his own upbringing by building a family of his own and striving to provide them with everything he'd missed out on as a kid.

Rand's experience seemed to have had the opposite effect. He avoided family, preferring a single, solitary life. His quietness, his reserve, his lack of athletic skills nearly every American male developed at a young age all pointed back to the fact that his mother and father had had very little, if any, influence on his life.

With her thoughts centered on Rand, she shifted her gaze to look at him. He stood tall beside Jack, appearing handsome and dignified in a dark pin-striped suit, Lila cradled in the curve of one arm. If a person were judging by exterior appearances, they'd never suspect the deprivation of his youth, but Cecile knew it was all there, carefully hidden.

At the moment Rand's attention was fixed on the minister, absorbing each and every word said. The guy took everything so seriously, Cecile knew without a doubt he'd be able to recite the entire ceremony to her later verbatim, if asked.

At the thought, a giggle bubbled up and she quickly hid it behind a cough. Rand glanced her way. His left eyebrow, as always, was arched a shade higher than the right, which made his expression seem even more serious and daunting.

She remembered the first time she'd seen him, standing opposite her over Malinda's hospital bed, he'd worn just such an expression. She'd thought him egotistical, a playboy. Later that same day she'd discovered something else in his eyes. Compassion. The temptation to knuckle under and accept his comfort had been there before she could stop it. But she had managed not to respond to the temptation. She had run, just like she always did, for she'd learned the hard way never to depend on anyone but herself for comfort.

But since then, she'd discovered that compassion was more than a facial expression for Rand. It was a quality he wore bone deep. For along with compassion, he offered understanding, support—and best of all, himself.

A butterfly took flight in her stomach as she gazed into warm, brown eyes. Sunbeams slanted through the stained-glass window behind him, their golden shafts of light piercing him and giving him a mystical, almost celestial appearance. He looked calm, relaxed, and as cool and inviting as an oasis.

Odd, since Cecile herself felt as if her body were on fire.

She tried to smile at him, but her lips felt stiff and parched. Wetting them, she tried again, and a soft smile trembled forth. He smiled back before he returned his attention to the minister. That simple look from him turned Cecile's knees to jelly.

She shifted the baby in her arms, but found she couldn't look away from Rand. And who could? The man was drop-dead handsome, with a face designed to make women pant. His face was a mixture of fascinating angles—square jaw, sharp cheekbones, a chin with the slightest hint of a cleft. And if his face wasn't enough to bring a woman to her knees, the rest of his body could certainly do the trick.

Unfortunately, Cecile had more than just the sight of him to draw this assumption. She had memories to justify her claim. Shoulders broad and strong, curved just right to cradle a woman's head. And his chest ... oh, God, yes, his chest. Muscular and comforting, a combination Cecile found hard to resist. Dusted with dark hair and padded with muscle, his chest rose above a stomach with a topography matching that of a six-pack. Though concealed behind his suit trousers, she vividly remembered the strength of his legs. When they'd made love, he had wound them around hers and gently guided her to more intimate positions in a lovers' dance that had her all but purring her pleasure.

She had to give him credit. The guy was one hell of a lover. Gentle, without being timid. Virile, without being demanding.

A sigh built in her chest and quickly she stiffened, putting starch in her knees to keep from swooning like a love-sick teenager. No! she told herself at the tightness she felt building in her chest and throat. What she was feeling was simply admiration and respect, not love. Rand Coursey was kind, generous and intelligent, all characteristics she'd find admirable in any man. The fact that he was a skilled lover was simply icing on the cake.

She forced herself to slowly exhale and her breath rattled out of her. Just because she recognized all those traits and admired them, didn't mean she was falling in love with him.

Theirs was a physical relationship, she told herself sternly. Strictly physical, nothing more. Flattening her lips in determination, she tore her gaze from Rand and made herself focus on the minister.

Gradually the tightening in her chest receded and her breathing became easier. Relieved to see that she was back in control, she allowed a half smile to curve at her lips. Yep, theirs was clearly a physical relationship, all right...and one she intended to enjoy to its fullest.

"Looks like your brunch is a success."

The tickle of Rand's breath at her ear had Cecile half turning, a smile building as her shoulder bumped the solid wall of his chest. The fact that she could look at him, touch him and talk to him without experiencing the swooning sensations the mere sight of him at the church had produced, pleased her enormously. "It is, isn't it?"

One willing to give credit where credit was due, she set the empty quiche dish she'd just picked up right back on the table to slip an arm around his waist. "But I couldn't have done it without you." She rose to her tiptoes and planted a kiss on his cheek. "Thanks."

When she would have turned away to finish clearing the buffet table, Rand placed a hand at her waist, holding her at his side. "Try that again, only this time a little lower and to the left," he whispered just loud enough for her to hear.

"Oh, you." Cecile gave his chest a playful shove, but Rand only pulled her closer. The look in his eyes told her he might be teasing, but the passion was there, carefully banked. Batting her eyes seductively, Cecile tipped her face up to his. "Why, Dr. Coursey, I do believe you're trying to seduce me."

"Since when do you need seducing?"

Before she could reply, he dipped his head and quickly took her mouth in a breath-robbing kiss. His lips were cool at first contact, but quickly warmed, spreading a responding heat through Cecile. Her hands tightened against his chest, gathering his shirt's starched fabric within her fingers.

Physical, she reminded herself as her stockinged toes curled into the plush carpet. Strictly physical.

But her internal reminder couldn't stop the sudden roar in her ears or the flutter in her stomach, which was quickly working its way up her chest. It didn't help that he had unobtrusively slipped a hand from her waist to cup her behind. Never had a man taken her so far so quickly.

"Mama?"

CeeCee's voice sounded as if it came from a hundred miles away. "Hmm?" she murmured against Rand's lips.

"Malinda said I could hold one of the twins if a grown-up helps me."

Cecile managed to drag her lips from Rand's but only found the strength to draw far enough away to rest her forehead against his chest. "In a minute, CeeCee," she said, struggling for air.

"Please, Mama? Malinda said she's gonna have to feed them in a minute and then they'll go to sleep."

"Not right now, sweetheart. I've got to finish clearing the table so I can set out the desserts." And she'd do that as soon as she found the strength to lift her head from the irresistible warmth of Rand's chest.

"Will I qualify as a grown-up?"

The vibration of Rand's voice rumbling through his chest had Cecile lifting her head to look at him. He smiled down at her. "I'm over twenty-one and extremely mature for my age. And I have had tons of experience holding babies."

Another example of his unending kindness and understanding. And this one directed to her child, which endeared him to Cecile in a way Rand would never appreciate, even if she wanted to explain. Cecile moved back a step, unable to stop the smile that tugged at her lips. "All right, then, I guess you'll do."

Rand dropped his gaze to CeeCee, who stood, nearly bursting with excitement, at his side. He held out his hand. "There you have it, CeeCee. A consenting grown-up at your service." Giggling, CeeCee caught his hand and quickly dragged him to the living room and Malinda's side.

Cecile shook her head, chuckling softly as she picked up the quiche dish. The man was simply too good to be true.

It took her four trips to clear the table and another two to replenish it with the desserts Rand had whipped up the night before. He'd done a wonderful job. Each dessert was a work of art, and the nibbles she'd sneaked in the kitchen proved they tasted as good as they looked.

She brushed at a crumb littering the linen cloth—the one Rand had insisted on ironing. She chuckled, remembering their debate over whether the cloth required pressing. The man was obsessive, at best.

Shaking her head, Cecile began to align the dessert forks beside the stack of crystal plates. She heard CeeCee laugh and glanced up. Her daughter sat on the sofa in the living room cradling one of the twins in her arms. Rand sat beside her, a hand tucked protectively beneath the baby's head to support it. His own head was tipped close to CeeCee's, a half smile lifting one corner of his mouth while he listened to her excited chatter.

Cecile's chest tightened and her throat threatened to close at the sight. Her hands grew slick with perspiration and she wiped them down the sides of her dress. Oh, Lord, no, she thought desperately. Not again. The tightness in her chest and throat, dry mouth, sweaty palms...the same symptoms she'd experienced at the church. I must be getting sick, she told herself, but instinctively raised her thumb to her mouth and found the nail.

What were CeeCee and Rand talking and laughing about? And why was her daughter being so friendly with Rand, anyway? No one knew better than Cecile what a hard nut to crack CeeCee was when it came to allowing a man to get near—with the exception of Cecile's father, of course. But just look at her. Wearing a grin wide enough to split her face and chattering away like a magpie. She'd never given any of the other men Cecile had allowed into their home the time of day. Why Rand?

The question made her uneasy.

"With all this good food in front of you, why feast on a thumbnail?"

Cecile jerked her thumb from her mouth, guiltily folded it into her palm and curled her fingers around it. She cut a glance at Malinda and graced her friend with a frown.

Malinda simply smiled. "Sweet, aren't they?"

Not wanting to admit she knew who Malinda was talking about, Cecile busied her fingers by realigning the silverware she'd just laid out. "Who's sweet?"

Malinda nodded her head in the direction of the sofa. "Rand and CeeCee." Unwillingly, Cecile glanced their way.

"She's been trailing him ever since he arrived. I think she's smitten."

"Yeah, well," Cecile said dryly, "you know CeeCee. She's a sucker for older men."

"Really? I thought she only had room in her heart for your dad?" She chuckled softly when Rand smoothed CeeCee's bangs from her eyes. "I think Rand is equally infatuated."

"Who wouldn't be?" Cecile replied, slapping a fork down on the table a little harder than necessary. "When CeeCee turns on the charm, she's hard to resist."

"True," Malinda replied thoughtfully. "But she seems to genuinely like Rand. Maybe she sees him as a father figure or something."

A father figure? Cecile frowned, narrowing her eyes, trying to see what Malinda saw.

Malinda chuckled and patted Cecile's arm. "Would you listen to me? I sound like an armchair psychologist." She waved a hand as if to brush away the subject, then dipped her head over a strawberry pie heaped high with whipped cream. She closed her eyes and inhaled deeply. "Smells absolutely sinful, and here I stand with a good ten pounds more to lose." She draped an arm around Cecile's shoulders. "You know, when you offered to have this brunch, I was a bit worried."

"Well, thanks."

Malinda squeezed her to her side. "Let's face it, Cecile. Cooking is certainly not your cup of tea. But everything is simply delicious! You've done a wonderful job."

Cecile deepened her frown, wanting to lie but knowing she couldn't. "I didn't. Rand did."

"Excuse me?"

"Rand made the quiche. And the muffins. And the cheese grits." She flipped a hand at the carved melon still piled high with fresh fruit. "He carved the melon for the centerpiece and prepared the fruit, too." Her hand lighted on the linen tablecloth and she brushed away a pastry crumb. "He even ironed the tablecloth."

"Sounds like a keeper to me."

Cecile rolled her eyes, even though her heart fluttered at the thought. "Don't get any ideas."

"Oh, I wouldn't dream of it. Especially since the two of you seem to be handling things so well all by yourselves." Malinda plucked a strawberry from the top of the whipped cream and took a delicate bite.

Horrified by what her friend had just said, Cecile stared at her. "What do you mean by that?"

"I saw the look in his eyes every time he glanced your way during the christening."

Cecile's mouth fell open. She hadn't seen that.

"I also saw the kiss CeeCee interrupted." Malinda arched a brow Cecile's way and puckered her lips, looking smug.

"No, I'd say the two of you don't need any help from an old matchmaker like me." She snagged another strawberry and licked the whipped cream from it. "Although I am surprised, considering Rand's a doctor and all." Deciding she'd worry about the calories later, she popped the berry into her mouth and shrugged her shoulders. "But then, who would have thought I'd fall in love with Jack?"

"Love?" Cecile repeatedly stupidly. "Who said anything about love?"

Before Malinda could reply, Madison, the twin CeeCee held, began to cry. Rand glanced up, searching for and finding Malinda. He mouthed the words, "I think she's hungry."

"Duty calls." Malinda hugged Cecile to her side before hurrying away.

Cecile watched Malinda take the baby from CeeCee, then widened her eyes when Rand stood, stretched out his hands and hauled CeeCee up into his arms. CeeCee hated being treated like a baby, yet she slung her arm around Rand's neck and pressed her cheek to his.

A father figure? No, Cecile told herself, and made herself turn away. CeeCee wasn't looking for a father figure. She was just a friendly kid and demonstrative with her affection when she liked someone. And what wasn't there to like about Rand?

Cecile closed the door behind the last guest and then fell back against it, jutting out her lower lip to blow up at her bangs. Finally her duties as hostess were over.

"Tired?"

Cecile didn't even try to hide her fatigue. "Exhausted. How about you?" she asked as she pushed away from the door. She wound an arm around Rand's waist as they both headed for the living room.

"A little."

At the sight of all the dirty plates and cups scattered about and the yards of pastel ribbon and wrapping paper littering the floor, Cecile groaned.

Rand squeezed her shoulder reassuringly. "Don't worry. I'll help with the cleanup."

"I vote we skip cleanup and take a nap in the sun by the pool while the kids swim."

Rand clicked his tongue, admonishing her for the suggestion. "I vote we all chip in, clean up the mess, *then* take a nap by the pool."

"We all chip in, as in, you and me?"

"The kids can help."

"They can?" she asked doubtfully, fully aware of her children's aversion to anything associated with housework.

"Sure." Rand put his thumb and little finger in his mouth and let out a piercing whistle that Cecile was sure would have every dog in the neighborhood howling. Within seconds—and much to Cecile's surprise—all three of her children came running into the living room.

Dent was first to arrive. "What's going on?"

"Cleanup."

Dent looked at Rand as if he had a screw loose or something. "So?"

"So, grab the vacuum cleaner." He turned to Gordy. "You can start taking all the dirty dishes to the kitchen."

CeeCee tugged on Rand's sleeve. "What about me?"

"You, my little angel," he said, scooping her up and tossing her high into the air, making her squeal. "Are in charge of gathering and bagging all the wrapping paper and ribbons. I think I saw an empty sack on the center island in the kitchen. You can use it to put the trash in."

CeeCee skipped off, obviously delighted to do Rand's bidding. Dent and Gordy didn't budge so much as an inch.

"Don't you boys want to go swimming?"

"Yeah."

"And don't you need an adult present in order to do that?"

"Yeah."

"Well, then, I'd say you better get cracking. Otherwise, there won't be any swimming today."

Throughout this entire dialogue, Cecile simply stood, too stunned to do anything but listen. Nobody told her children what to do but her. Others, like Josh, had tried, and sent the kids into fits of rebellion that took her weeks to iron out. As a result, she was extremely protective about parenting and reserved that responsibility strictly for herself.

When the boys turned to her, waiting for her to interfere or to tell them it was all a joke, that they weren't really expected to help, the words were right there on the tip of her tongue to tell them just that. But before she could utter the first word, Gordy picked up a plate, then another, and shuffled off to the kitchen.

To her further astonishment, Dent heaved a frustrated breath, then mumbled, "Where's the vacuum?"

She quickly swallowed her retort.

With everyone helping, the house was put back in order in record time. Cecile reflected on this novelty while she lay on her stomach in a lounge chair by the pool fresh from a nap, watching Rand and the kids playing a game of Marco Polo in the water.

The game was one of the children's favorites, and one she herself played with them often. She'd even talked Josh into joining them once, but he had been unwilling to compensate for the age difference between himself and the kids and had spoiled the fun of the game with his competitiveness.

Rand, on the other hand, didn't seem to mind losing to someone half his size and twenty or more years his junior.

In fact, he seemed to share their excitement when they found him, thus winning the game.

Cecile knew it wasn't fair to compare, but she couldn't help thinking Rand's willingness and acceptance of defeat made him a bigger winner than Josh.

When she arrived at this conclusion, her gaze was fixed on Rand, who had just settled himself on the steps at the shallow end of the pool. Sunlight caught the droplets of water beading his shoulders and chest, turning them to diamonds. She watched as he combed his hair back, his fingers leaving narrow furrows through rich, brown hair darkened by the water. His biceps bulged at the action, then lengthened as he reached his hands high over his head and stretched. The play of muscle across his chest and midsection made shivers chase down Cecile's spine.

He glanced in her direction, his gaze settling on her. A slow smile tipped one corner of his mouth. He stood, water dripping from his body, and stepped from the pool. Ambling her way, he snagged a towel from the back of a chair and rubbed at his hair, then his chest. At the foot of her lounge chair he stopped, still grinning.

"Have a nice nap?"

Swallowing back the emotions the sight of him drew, she murmured, "Perfect." Returning his smile, she raised her knees and tucked her feet close to her bottom to give him room to sit down. "Did you?"

"Couldn't sleep."

"I'm sorry," she said sympathetically. "Were the kids too loud?"

"No. They were having too much fun. Made me so envious I decided to join them." He sat down, his back to her, then leaned back, shouldering her knees apart until his head rested between her breasts. He tilted his head back, until their gazes met. "I think I'm in love."

Cecile's eyes widened in panic. "What!"

Rand chuckled, lowering his chin to nod at the kids splashing about in the pool. He laced his fingers over his chest. "With CeeCee. She's a little angel."

Cecile placed a hand over her heart. He'd scared her there for a minute. She'd thought he'd meant he was in love with her, in which case she would have been forced to send him packing.

"Did she tell you I chased the monster out of her room last night?"

Not aware of this, Cecile looked at him in surprise. "No, but then there wasn't much time for idle chitchat this morning. We all had to hit the ground running in order to make it to the church on time."

He chuckled again, his shoulders brushing against her knees. "She was so cute, standing there in the utility room, hugging her baby doll. I tried to get her to go back to bed by telling her he was probably gone, but she insisted the monster wouldn't go away unless you chased it out from under her bed." He tipped his head back, meeting her gaze once again. Laughter sparkled in his eyes. "It took some fast talking to convince her that I was mean enough to take care of the job for you."

Cecile smiled in spite of herself. Rand mean? She didn't blame CeeCee for doubting him. Personally, she didn't think the man capable of such an emotion. "And were you?"

"Did she come and wake you and ask you to take care of it for her?"

"No."

"Then I guess I was mean enough."

She ruffled his hair, then gave in to the urge to drop a kiss on his forehead. "That's good to know, because in the future I'll call *you* when CeeCee awakens me at three in the morning, wanting me to slay her monsters for her."

"A monster slayer," he said thoughtfully, his gaze still locked on hers. He lifted a hand to her cheek. "Does this job offer any fringe benefits?"

A smile tugged at Cecile's mouth. Rand found the center of a dimple with the tip of his finger, sending lightning bolts ripping clear to Cecile's toes. "Maybe," she said coyly. "What did you have in mind?"

"You."

Cecile took one look at CeeCee's face and said, "Don't even ask."

"Oh, but, Mama, he's so cute."

Cecile turned her back on her daughter and the bag of fur perched on his haunches beside her and began stuffing baseball equipment into the canvas bag. She couldn't and wouldn't be suckered in by CeeCee's pitiful expression or the mutt's forlorn eyes.

"Babies are cute, dog's are a pain the rear," she said without displaying a shred of compassion.

"I'll feed him every day and take him for walks and give him baths. You won't have to do a thing, Mama, I promise."

"I've heard that story before," she said dryly.

"Ple-e-ease, Mama? Pretty please with sugar on it?"

Cecile cinched up the top of the bag and heaved a frustrated breath as she straightened. She was going to have to be tough, for CeeCee was hard to resist when she really turned on the charm.

But before she could reply, a cold, wet nose nuzzled the back of her knee.

"Oh, Mama, look! He likes you!"

Grimacing, Cecile twisted around to scowl at the dog. "He doesn't like me. He's probably hungry." She waved a hand at him. "Just look at the size of this beast."

The dog obviously mistook her gesture for an invitation because he reared on his hind legs, planting his front paws on Cecile's chest. The unexpected weight knocked Cecile to the ground and before she could react, the dog was on top of her, licking her face.

"Get off me, you big lug!" she cried as she shoved at his chest, craning her neck to avoid his wet, raspy tongue. "CeeCee, for heaven's sake, call this mutt off."

"Shaggy! No! Down, boy!"

"Problem?"

Cecile glanced over the top of the dog's head to see Rand standing above her. "Yes. Get this beast off me."

Rand caught the dog by the scruff of the neck and hauled him to his side. Immediately, CeeCee dropped to her knees beside them, her arms locked tight around the animal's neck. "It's okay, Shaggy," she murmured consolingly. "Mama didn't mean to scare you."

"Scare *him!*" Cecile cried indignantly.

Chuckling, Rand extended a hand to help Cecile to her feet. "I didn't know ya'll had a dog."

"We *don't*," she said as she angrily brushed dirt from her backside. "He showed up while we were practicing, and CeeCee's been playing with him. Now she wants to take the beast home." Having dealt with the dirt as best she could, she turned her foul mood on Rand. "And where were you? Did you forget we had an extra practice before the game?"

"No, I didn't forget. I had an emergency delivery. I tried to call you from the hospital, but you'd already left." He cupped a hand behind her neck and gently massaged. "Did you miss me?" he asked teasingly.

"No," she grumbled, trying to hold on to her anger. But the soothing ministrations of his hand on her tensed neck muscles made her weaken. "But I could have used another set of hands and lungs at practice."

"Did the boys give you a hard time?"

She closed her eyes on a sigh and let her head fall back against his hand. "No, not really. They're just keyed up about the game. We're playing the Royals, and they're undefeated. The boys want to beat them in the worst sort of way."

"And we will."

Cecile opened her eyes to frown at him. "How can you be so sure?"

He winked at her, smiling a secretive smile. "Because today I feel lucky, that's why." He hefted the bag of equipment. "Come on, CeeCee, and bring Fido. Since he's going to be a member of the family, he can be the team mascot." The three headed for the playing field, with CeeCee skipping along beside Rand while the dog trotted after them.

Cecile stared after them, her mouth gaped wide. *A member of the family?* She hadn't said anything about CeeCee being allowed to keep that dog! "Hey! Wait a minute," she called after them. "We're not keeping that dog."

"Sure you are," Rand yelled over his shoulder. "He'll make a great watchdog."

Glaring at his back, she tightened her hands into fists at her side, feeling outmaneuvered. And nobody outmaneuvered Cecile Kingsley. She stalked after them, her anger back and the muscles in her neck tensed again.

By the sixth inning, Cecile's mood had improved dramatically. She'd forgotten all about the dog, her determination not to take it home and her irritation with Rand for setting the seed in CeeCee's mind that the beast was already a member of the family.

Her memory lapse was probably due to the fact that the White Sox were leading the Royals by four runs. The players were convinced that Shaggy—the official team mascot now, thanks to Rand—was a good-luck charm and each made a point to rub the dog's head before taking their turn at bat.

Cecile wasn't one who believed in luck—she'd never personally had any other than the bad variety—but her attitude toward the dog gradually began to soften. Even when she nearly tripped over the beast as she was leaving the dugout, she refused to lose her temper. If the boys thought the dog was a good-luck charm, who was she to argue the point? They were playing better than they ever had before and looked like they were headed for a win.

A win for the White Sox, she mused, the Little League's underdog team. And against the Royals at that!

The crowd seemed to share Cecile's enthusiasm. The bleachers were full of family and friends of the players, munching popcorn and sipping sodas while they rooted for their favorite team. The die-hard fans lined the chain-link fence from the dugout to the bleachers, sitting in lawn chairs or on quilts spread on the ground.

From her position beside first base, Cecile watched Dent step up to the plate and felt the swell of parental pride. The score was about to increase by one, she was sure. She knew this because she could see the glint of determination in her son's eye.

The first pitch came in high and outside. Dent watched it sail by without blinking an eye. That's my boy, she thought with pride. Make the pitcher pitch to you. The pitcher wound up for the second pitch and threw the ball hard. From Cecile's viewpoint it looked like it was going to be high and inside—Dent's favorite kind. He swung hard, meeting the ball with the bat and sending it shooting high in the air... but foul. As usual, the cry of "Heads up!" went up from the crowd.

Unfortunately, two young mothers sitting in lawn chairs by the fence, who were engrossed in conversation and oblivious to the events on the field, didn't hear the warning and continued to gossip away, their heads tipped toward each other.

Rand watched the ball's descent from his position at third base. When it became obvious the ball was headed straight for the women and they weren't moving, he bolted for the fence. He sunk the toe of one sneaker halfway up the chain-link meshing and his fingers on the top rail, hauling himself over. He leaned and snagged the ball bare-handed, just shy of one of the women's head.

The crowd cheered, but no one louder than Cecile. Winded from the exertion, Rand jumped down, held the ball up so she could see it, and took a bow. Cecile laughed, clapping her hands at his antics. When the crowd settled, a female voice from the bleachers yelled, "Way to go, Rand. You're still my hero."

Cecile whipped her head around. A woman—a very young woman—a very *beautiful*, young woman—was standing, waving at Rand. Cecile felt the bottom fall out of her stomach. *Still my hero?* Is that what she had said? Cecile stared at her, slowly becoming aware of the nurse's uniform the woman wore. Still smiling and waving, the nurse wove her way through the tangle of people crowding the bleachers.

Then he was there beside her. Rand. Hauling the woman into his arms, laughing, squeezing her against his chest.

Then he kissed her.

Sickened, Cecile closed her eyes against the sight and turned away. She wanted to go home. She wanted to hide.

She wanted to throw up. But she couldn't. She had a game to finish. The boys were counting on her.

And why did it matter if Rand kissed a hundred women, anyway? It wasn't as if she were in love with him or anything. Theirs was a physical relationship, strictly physical. She'd established the rules herself.

Sucking in a deep, fortifying breath, she opened her eyes. Another deep breath and she found the strength to signal the umpire to resume the game.

No, she didn't care who Rand Coursey kissed, she told herself as she forced her focus on Dent preparing for the next pitch. And if, perchance, she discovered she did care, Rand Coursey would never know it. Of that, she was certain.

Eight

Cecile strode into Rand's bedroom, kicked off a sneaker and sent it flying. The second sneaker quickly followed. "I still don't know how you swung this."

Chuckling, Rand picked up the sneakers and aligned them neatly at the foot of the bed. Cecile had only been in his bedroom one other time, and this visit was proving to be much like the first—she entered stripping. "I told you I was feeling lucky tonight."

"Yeah, but luck's one thing, unloading three kids for a whole night is quite another." She caught the hem of her T-shirt and jerked upward.

Proud of himself and the plan he'd evolved, Rand smiled. "I made a bet with Jack. I told him if we won the game, he had to take your kids for the weekend."

"And if we'd lost?" she asked, tugging the T-shirt over her head and shaking her hair free.

Rand winced, reminded of the consequences if the score hadn't gone his way. "Well, let's just say instead of three kids underfoot tonight, we'd have had nine."

With her shorts shoved to her knees, Cecile glanced up. "You mean, you promised to take all of the Brannan kids overnight if we lost the game?"

"That was the bet."

Slowly, Cecile stepped out of the shorts, then hugged them to her breasts as she looked at him, suspicion building. "And you were planning on handling all six of the Brannan kids, including the twins, by yourself?"

"Well, sort of," he said sheepishly. "I was counting on your help."

"Oh, so you included me in on your bet?" She lifted the shorts to throw them at him, but Rand caught her hand midair.

"Seemed only fair, especially considering if I won, then you'd win, as well." He wrapped his arms around her waist, her shorts dangling from his fingers to tickle her bare rear end.

"How's that?" she asked, forgiving him because she was exactly where she wanted to be.

"You get a night away from the children, and we get an opportunity to be alone."

"And who said I wanted to be alone with you?" she teased, rubbing her breasts against his chest.

"Are you always this disagreeable?"

"Only when I'm being manipulated."

"If I promise to ask your permission before obligating you to anything in the future, will you forgive me?"

She'd long since done that. But she wouldn't tell Rand. It was much more fun to tease him. "I don't know. Especially since you saddled me with that beast of a dog."

"You wanted that dog as badly as CeeCee. You're just too stubborn to admit it."

The fact that he was right made her smile. "You think you're pretty smart, don't you, Coursey?"

"Brilliant."

She placed a fingertip in the cleft of his chin and lifted her face to meet his gaze. Lightning struck and thunder rolled at the contact.

Rand tightened his grip, desire for her already churning within him. "How about a shower? You scrub my back, I'll scrub yours?"

"You got yourself a deal, Coursey."

Hot steam billowed around them, misting their bodies and turning their skin a healthy rose. Her hands slickened with soap, Cecile moved around Rand in a shower obviously built for two, rubbing, massaging and thoroughly enjoying the feel of his skin warming beneath her palms.

The scent of the soap wafted beneath her nose, teasing her with the fragrance of herbs and wildflowers. Inhaling deeply, she mentally forced each muscle in her tense body to relax under the pulsating spray beating down on her until only one tensed muscle remained. And that muscle was the one that wouldn't allow Cecile to forget about the nurse she'd seen in Rand's arms at the game. Sighing, she turned him away from her so she could focus on his back.

Obviously enjoying the attention, Rand cocked a knee and braced both hands against the tiled wall. "Do you hire out?"

Cecile smiled in spite of her troubled thoughts. "No. Strictly a barter situation. My turn's next."

Her thoughts once again returned to the nurse. Gathering the bar of soap between her hands, she bit her bottom lip as she lathered more soap between her palms. *I wonder if that woman ever shared this shower with Rand?* Rolling her eyes at her own jealousy, she slapped her hands to his back.

"Whoa," he said, edging away from the increased pressure. "Easy does it."

"Sorry." Though she gentled her touch, her thoughts remained on that other woman. "Rand?"

"Hmm?"

"Who was that woman at the ballpark?"

He turned his head slightly, but not far enough to meet Cecile's gaze. "What woman?"

Irritated, Cecile slapped a hand against his back, digging her fingertips into his shoulder muscles and making him flinch. "Sorry," she said, gentling her touch once again. "The woman you kissed."

"Oh, her." Rand faced the wall again and dipped his head, giving her easier access to his neck. "Just a friend."

"Oh? Must be a pretty good friend." Cecile heard the jealousy in her tone and quickly added, "Not that I mind, of course."

Rand glanced down, but all he could see was the top of Cecile's head as she stooped to furiously work at his lower back. If she rubbed any harder, he suspected he wouldn't have much skin left. He bit back a smile as he realized the reason behind her roughness. "No, I'm sure you don't," he said softly. "But, no, I usually don't greet friends that way, but Marcia is special. More like a sister than a friend."

Cecile paused, her fingers going still. She'd heard that one before—from her husband, Denton. He, too, had claimed a mere platonic friendship when she'd caught him red-handed in a questionable situation with a woman.

Frowning, she glanced up to find Rand looking down at her. The brown eyes that met hers were open and honest and warmed by understanding, not at all like Denton's. Looking into Denton's eyes had been like looking into a void. He was excellent at turning his gaze expressionless, thus hiding his guilt.

But not Rand. His eyes were filled with emotion. Understanding. Compassion. Passion. Tearing her gaze away, she mentally shook herself, riddled with guilt for comparing the two. Rand was not Denton. If he said the woman was a friend, she was just that. A friend.

And what did it matter, anyway? she asked herself as she moved her hands to the cheeks of his butt and gently massaged, pleased when she won a groan of pleasure from Rand. There were no strings attached to their relationship. They were friends—lovers, yes, but nothing more.

Rand twisted around, taking her by surprise, and squatted down to put his eyes on a level with hers. Slowly he caught her hand in his and took the soap into his own. The heat from his eyes burned into her own. "Your turn," he said, his voice husky with promise. Catching her hand in his, he rose, pulling her to stand before him.

Holding her with nothing but the power of his gaze, he dropped the soap to the shower floor. Bubbles foamed, tickling her feet as he laid his hands on her shoulders. He smoothed them in a lazy, bone-melting journey to her neck. With an unerring sense, his skilled fingers sought and found that one muscle that had remained tense.

Suspecting he knew the reason behind her tension, Rand maneuvered until the muscle lay between his thumb and finger, then gently began to knead away the tautness.

"She really is just a friend, Cecile. I'd never lie to you."

He knew, just like he always did, exactly what she was thinking. Unable to stand the heat in his gaze any longer, Cecile closed her eyes, letting her head fall back against the tiled wall. Tears burned behind her closed lids at the sincerity in his voice. Swallowing back the emotion, she felt that last muscle go lax.

Rand felt it, too, and experienced a sense of relief. He wanted nothing between himself and Cecile tonight.

Well, almost nothing, he thought on a silent laugh.

Finding the feminine curve of her throat irresistible, Rand pressed his lips there, felt the quickening in her pulse, then slid them down, his tongue licking at the droplets of water on her skin. His hands matched his lips' downward movement, from her shoulders to her lower back, then swept quickly upward to catch the weight of her breasts in his cupped palms. Groaning, he buried his face in the valley between her breasts.

Cecile sucked in a sharp breath as pulsations of exquisite pleasure ricocheted through her body. Steam continued to billow around her, hot needles of water to prick at her bared skin, but Cecile was aware of nothing but the feel of Rand against her. More than anything, she wanted to taste him.

Filling her fists with his hair, she lifted his head until his gaze once more leveled with hers. Framing his face with her hands, she closed her eyes and leaned into him, finding his lips and moaning her satisfaction at the passion she tasted there. This is what she'd hungered for, the taste of him, the possessive feel of his lips on her.

But more, she wanted to erase the taste and memory of another woman's lips there.

Satisfied she'd done that, she discovered a deeper hunger, one that had nothing to do with anyone but Rand and her need for him. Wrapping her arms tight around his neck, she plastered her wet, soap-slickened body against his, desperate to satisfy this need for closeness. With an innate understanding Cecile would never tire of or fully understand, Rand tightened his arms around her and pulled her off her feet.

Sliding a hand down her thigh, he caught her just below the knee and lifted her higher, groaning when her pelvic rasped against the swell of his manhood. He wrapped her legs low on his hips, then hitched her higher still until Cecile felt the thrust of his hardness at her most feminine core. Iron against velvet. Heat melding heat. The combining sensations added fire to a desire already raging out of control.

Taking a cautious step on the soap-slickened tile floor, Rand flattened her back against the shower wall. With the cheeks of her butt cupped in his hands, he lowered her, slowly, letting her honeyed cream lubricate their joining.

Once he was buried deep within her, he pressed his forehead to hers, his chest rising and falling in deep, heaving breaths against her breasts. Then he moved, withdrawing in a painstaking slowness, until just the tip of his shaft remained within. Cecile cried out as needles of sensation burst within her, duplicating those of the water stinging her face.

Unable to stand the anticipation a moment longer, she arched against him, taking him in, swallowing the cry of sheer pleasure that bubbled forth. She rode him, her head flung back, water rivering down her face, her fingers digging into shoulders wide enough and strong enough to carry the weight of the world. Desire built until she thought she couldn't bear another second of this sweet torture, but she refused to take the final plunge without Rand with her.

"Now, Cecile," he whispered against her breasts. "Now!" Her response was a low, guttural cry as she arched against him, absorbing the pulsating throbs as spasms shook his body, matching those that pulsed deep within her.

On a ragged sigh, she dropped her forehead to his shoulder and clung to him while the water continued to pelt their skin.

* * *

He woke to find her face only inches from his. To see her there, in his bed, sleeping so peacefully, pleased Rand in a way he hadn't expected. That his usual Sunday routine would be broken didn't phase him. He'd planned this. He'd made a wild wager—him, a man who never gambled on anything, much less a Little League ball game—with his friend Jack to pull it off. And he'd won. The thought had a smile pushing at the corners of his mouth. The prize was certainly worth what he had always considered a sin.

Twenty-four uninterrupted hours with Cecile. That in itself was no small accomplishment. The woman lived in a frenzy of activity. With her three children and all their demands on her time, her duties as baseball coach and her responsibilities at the children's clothing store she shared in partnership with Malinda, the lady had precious little time to spare.

And he'd always thought he maintained a full schedule. He chuckled softly. The demands of his medical practice paled in comparison to the schedule Cecile kept.

He lifted his head and propped his cheek on his palm to study her. Her lips were slightly parted and puckered just the tiniest bit. Tangled tresses of honey blond hair silvered by moonlight spilled over her shoulder, but fell just short of covering her breasts. Her left hand cushioned her cheek between the pillow while her right was buried somewhere underneath its downy folds.

Softened by sleep, but still rosy from their lovemaking, a budded nipple winked up at Rand. The temptation to reach out and touch it was so strong he had to force his hand into a fist to keep from doing just that.

Asleep, Cecile looked as fragile and innocent as CeeCee. He supposed it was because she wasn't talking. He muffled a chuckle against his forearm to keep from waking her. She was a talker, all right. And when she wasn't talking a blue streak, she was cussing one. So unlike the woman he'd expected to fall in love with.

And he did love her. He'd felt the feeling growing for weeks, but had ignored it. Or at least, he'd tried to. But he couldn't ignore it any longer. His feelings ran too deep and too strong to hide them from her much longer.

And that was the problem.

He frowned as he continued to stare at her. He'd made the deal with her. A strictly physical relationship, no strings attached. She'd even been so bold as to tell him that if he ever mentioned the word love, she was history. And he'd been fool enough to agree.

Granted, he'd had his reasons for conceding so readily to her list of contingencies. He hadn't wanted or thought he needed a family. Now he wondered how he'd ever live without them. Any of them. But especially CeeCee. He supposed it was her age or the fact that she was a little girl or maybe it was because she was outnumbered by her brothers. Whatever the reason, she'd stolen his heart as surely as her mother had. She'd accomplished this the first time he'd seen her, shuffling down the sidewalk, pushing the rickety baby carriage in front of her, tears brimming in her eyes. If that confrontation hadn't been enough to drag him to his knees, the night she'd asked him to slay her monster for her certainly had.

He couldn't remember ever feeling more needed...or more inadequate. But she'd accepted him, and so had the boys, though not as readily. He wondered if their mother ever would?

Needing to touch her, he caught a strand of hair and lifted it up and away from her face to lay a hand against her cheek. God, she was beautiful. And spirited. So much so that he feared what she'd say—or do, for that matter—if he found the nerve to tell her how much he cared.

Heaving a deep sigh, he dropped his head to the crook of his elbow and watched the woman he'd fallen in love with sleep, while he waited for dawn to bring a new day.

Cecile rolled over, her eyes still closed and patted the space beside her, searching for Rand. Her fingertips brushed only crisp linens. Squinting open her eyes, she looked and found the bed beside her empty. Sighing her disappointment, she reached for Rand's pillow and hugged it against her breasts. The crackle of paper beneath her hand had her scooting to a sitting position. A note was pinned to the linen pillowcase.

Cecile
Gone to the hospital to deliver a baby. Be back soon.
Make yourself at home.

                                                      Love, Rand

Love, Rand? Her fingers trembled slightly on the note as she sank back against the headboard, holding the crisp, white paper before her eyes. She touched the words, testing them as she read them aloud. "Love, Rand." She had a hard time pushing the word past the constriction in her throat. Love—even the mention of it—always made Cecile nervous.

He probably didn't mean anything by it, she told herself as she took the paper in one hand to fan her suddenly hot face. Not literally, anyway. Love was a salutation, meaningless simply in its overuse. But her reassurances didn't slow her heartbeat or dry the dampness on her palms or cool her flaming cheeks.

Love. She caught the edge of the paper between her teeth. She didn't like examining her feelings. She felt a lot safer just letting them hang out there in limbo unidentified. But she couldn't ignore this particular feeling any longer. Rand Coursey had gotten under her skin—and worse, wormed his way into her heart.

It wasn't as if she didn't recognize the feelings. She'd been in love before. Once. That relationship had left its scars. She'd loved Denton, scoundrel that he was. Of course, she hadn't known he was a scoundrel when she'd married him. All that had surfaced later—after the marriage certificate was signed, after her father had given him his medical practice and retired...and after she had given him her heart.

The memories hurt, but Cecile had long since learned to live with the pain. As a result of her experience with Denton, she didn't trust men and had resolved to never let one get close enough to hurt her again.

Unfortunately, Rand had burrowed in when she wasn't looking, and now he was so close she could feel his heartbeat as if it were her own. The thought frightened her, but not as much as she'd expected.

She kicked off the covers and sat up, stretching her hands high above her head. Maybe it was time to reevaluate her position. Maybe, just maybe, she should take a chance and tell Rand how she felt about him.

The thought made her freeze, her hands still stretched high above her head. She dropped them to her lap, her shoulders sagging. But Rand didn't want a family, she remembered, he'd told her so himself. "But that's ridiculous," she told the room as she hopped from the bed. If ever anyone needed a family, it was Rand Coursey. He was a natural father, patient and kind and generous to a fault.

She wasn't blind or stupid, either, for that matter. She'd seen him with CeeCee. And even her boys, rebels that they

were, responded well to him. She'd just have to convince
him of that, which shouldn't be a problem since she could
be just as persuasive as CeeCee when she turned on the
charm.

Her mind settled on the matter, she plucked the note from
the tangle of covers on the bed. *Make yourself at home,* she
read. She laughed and tossed the note over her shoulder.
"Thank you, Dr. Coursey. I believe I will," she replied as
she pulled her T-shirt over her head.

In the kitchen she found a banana and peeled it as she
strolled through his house, peeking into rooms. He was neat
to the point of obsession for not a thing was out of place.
His house was decorated expensively and with excellent
taste, but was vanilla in her estimation. There wasn't one
personal item in sight that revealed his personaiity or his
interests and not one of the rooms looked as if it were lived
in. So unlike her own home.

She took a bite of the banana as she strolled down the
hall. She stopped in front of the one door in the house she'd
found closed. She put a hand on the knob, but hesitated
when her conscience prodded, *You're snooping.*

"He said to make myself at home," she said, lifting her
chin defensively. She twisted the knob in her hand and
peeked inside. The room was obviously used as his study
and the only room she'd discovered so far that looked as if
he spent any time there.

"Okay, I'm snooping," she muttered under her breath as
she pushed the door open wide. Standing in the doorway,
she looked around.

The walls were paneled in a rich mahogany and lined with
bookshelves filled with books, art, and a library of video-
tapes. A television set was nestled among one of the shelves
and a huge, overstuffed chair and ottoman were aligned for
viewing a comfortable distance away. Feeling a little like

Goldilocks, Cecile tiptoed to the chair and sat down. Down-filled cushions ballooned around her, conforming to her shape. Liking the feel of the chair and the accompanying scent of Rand, she snuggled deeper and propped her bare feet on the ottoman.

Popping the last bite of banana into her mouth, she let the peel dangle from her fingers as she continued her inspection from the comfort of what she assumed to be Rand's favorite chair.

A desk with a computer, monitor, and telephone sat in front of the bookshelves, angled in such a way as to catch the morning light. Other than that, the desktop was clean as a whistle, which didn't surprise Cecile in the least. The man was, after all, a neatnik.

Spying a double frame on the table beside her chair, Cecile scooped it up. One side contained a picture of a young couple, obviously an old photo judging by the poor quality of the print and the way the couple were dressed. The other side framed a picture of a young boy, probably five or six, standing with a man and woman on either side of him. She looked closer and recognized the boy as Rand. She couldn't help but chuckle at the knobby knees and scrawny legs. He had his arm slung around both adults, pulling their faces close to his until the three were captured cheek-to-cheek.

Cecile felt tears burn behind her eyes. His parents. She knew this, because the likenesses were there. She touched the shallow cleft in the man's chin, which appeared smaller and less obvious in the boy's. The smile was his mother's, though. Open and friendly and totally endearing. She replaced the frame on the tabletop only to stare at it.

And Rand had said he didn't want a family. She brushed a tear from her eye and sniffed. Yeah, right. The man yearned for a family, he was just too stubborn—or too scared—to take a chance on one again. The fact that he kept a twenty-five-plus-year-old picture in the room where he spent the majority of his time told Cecile the picture as well as the memories were things he treasured.

The phone rang, and Cecile jumped, dropping the banana peel to the floor, startled by the unexpected noise. Should she answer it? She fretted over this for a moment and decided she should in the event that it was Rand calling. She stood and crossed to the desk, but as she reached for the phone, the answering machine clicked on.

Hitching a hip to the edge of the desk, she waited, listening to see if it was Rand. She chuckled at the solemness of his message, then waited for the click.

"Rand? It's Amber."

Her stomach knotted. Who in the hell was Amber? She stood and backed toward the door, her gaze fixed on the answering machine. Something told her she didn't want to hear this, but the sound of the voice followed her, rising in volume.

"I need your help." There was a pause in which Cecile could have sworn she heard a sob. She closed her hand over the doorknob, anxious to escape before she heard any more.

"I'm pregnant."

The words stopped Cecile cold, her hand clenched tight around the brass knob. *Pregnant?*

"You're the only one I can turn to. Rand, please, you've got to help me."

Cecile twisted the knob in her hand and bolted from the room, slamming the door behind her.

Though the door was closed, the sound of the voice carried through. "I know I promised to be careful, but...well, you know me. I love you, Rand. Please call me."

Cecile clapped her hands over her ears and ran, hot, angry tears spilling down her cheeks.

It didn't take long to collect her things from his bedroom. Even less to run to her car. Once there, she sank behind the steering wheel, fighting the nausea. She felt as if she were hanging, suspended in midair with one foot over a cliff and nothing below her but a long, hard fall. Thank God, she caught herself just short of falling off that cliff. If she hadn't heard that phone call...

No, she wouldn't let herself think about that. She *had* heard it, and as a result, saved herself the humiliation and heartbreak of telling Rand she had fallen in love with him.

Rand, I'm pregnant.

The snake! She twisted the key in the ignition and gunned the engine. He wasn't any different from any other man she'd met, only more convincing with his lies. She ripped the gearshift into reverse, wondering how many other children he'd fathered but failed to mention.

Nine

Rand whipped through traffic, taking the Kilpatrick Turn-
pike exit just east of Mercy Hospital at a speed totally out
of character for him. But he was in a hurry. For the first
time in his adult life—and a large portion of his youth—he
had a reason to go home...someone was there waiting for
him. The thought broadened the smile he wore and had
worn since awakening.

She was the first thing he'd seen when he'd opened his
eyes. Curled up next to him, a fist buried under her pillow,
thick velvety lashes curled against her cheeks. Her other arm
had been slung around his waist. There was something so
comforting in the gesture, so possessive. The mere thought
of it had a knot of emotion swelling in his chest.

He hoped she was still sleeping when he returned, for he
wanted her there in his bed, just as he'd left her. Sleeping
peacefully, cuddled around the pillow he had snugged up
against her when he'd slipped from the bed.

Throughout the delivery of an eight pound, six ounce bouncing baby boy, his thoughts had been centered on getting back to her. Crawling in bed with her, teasing her with kisses until she slowly awoke. She'd stretch and smile that slow, sensual smile, then she'd wrap her arms around his neck, pull him to her and they'd make love for hours.

She was such a passionate woman, both in and out of bed. If he spent the rest of his life trying, he knew he'd never get enough of her.

The thought made him ease his foot off the accelerator. *The rest of his life?* The exit for Western came up and he took it at a snail's pace. Perspiration beaded his forehead and he wiped at it with his forearm. *The rest of his life?*

He'd never had thoughts about spending the rest of his life with anyone. He frowned at himself in the rearview mirror. That was a lie. He'd harbored thoughts of marrying, but never a woman like Cecile.

Never a woman with children.

Home was less than two blocks away, yet Rand steered his car onto the shoulder. The car's air conditioner was set on maximum, yet perspiration dampened his shirt.

Calm down, Coursey, he told himself. You're a rational man, just think this through. He closed his eyes and mentally pictured them, Dent, Gordy and CeeCee, and tried to think how they'd react to having a man in their lives again.

CeeCee and he had already developed a pretty solid relationship, and she seemed to accept him without reservation.

As far as the boys were concerned, he didn't see any real problems with them, either. Gordy was a good kid with an inquisitive mind, much like Rand had been at that age. He needed encouragement and gentle direction to keep that sharp mind of his headed in the right direction. Since Rand understood the boy so well and shared his interests, he felt he was the perfect man to offer that guidance.

Now Dent was a different ball of wax altogether. The boy was very much like his mother, stubborn and headstrong, and of the three, seemed the most hesitant in accepting Rand. He supposed that reluctance was a result of the boy's age and probably the memories he carried of his dad. But Rand didn't want to take any of Dent's memories away from him. He simply wanted to add a few for the future.

He hauled in a deep breath and stared out the windshield as he slowly let it out. And he wanted a few memories of his own. A woman he loved to come home to every night, stepchildren to guide and nurture, and maybe if Cecile agreed, a child or two of their own making to round out their little family.

A car whipped by him, gently rocking his car, bringing him back from his mental wanderings.

"Man alive," he muttered under his breath, slowly coming to terms with the direction his heart—and thus his life—was heading. "How will I ever convince her to marry me?"

That thought plagued him as he pulled back into traffic and drove the rest of the way home. But by the time he reached the back door, anticipation had weakened his doubts.

"Cecile!" He walked through the back door, calling her name. When he didn't find her in the kitchen, he headed down the hall to the master bedroom where he'd left her hours before. The room was in shadows, but he could see that the bed was empty but for a tangle of sheets and scattered pillows.

"Cecile? Honey, I'm home!"

He strained, listening, and thought he heard the distant sound of the television. Cartoons. Figures, he thought with a smile. By the time he reached his study at the rear of the house, he had forgotten all about his doubts. He pushed open the door. His smile slowly faded when he saw that the television was on but the room was empty.

She probably grew tired of waiting and went home to shower and change, he told himself. He saw the message light blinking and crossed to his desk, thinking Cecile had more than likely called to tell him just that.

He punched the rewind button and waited, drumming his fingertips against the polished surface of his desk.

"Rand? It's Amber. I need your help."

His shoulders sagged at the sound of Amber's voice, already feeling the burden. He heard the muffled sob and let out a long sigh. What would it be this time? A traffic ticket she couldn't afford to pay? Money for her apartment rent? Her utilities had been shut off?

"I'm pregnant."

Rand closed his eyes on a groan and dropped his forehead to his palm. Pregnant. Jeez, Amber, what next?

"You're the only one I can turn to. Rand, please, you've got to help me." The desperation in her voice was something he was accustomed to hearing but he was moved by it, anyway. "I know I promised to be careful, but—" The laugh that followed was forced and bordered on hysteria. "Well, you know me." There was a sigh, then a touch of desperation edged her voice when she added, "I love you, Rand. Please call me."

The machine clicked, signaling the end of the message. Wearily, Rand leaned to push the rewind button. Pregnant. And she needed his help. Coming from Amber that could mean anything from a request for an abortion to a request for a sizable loan. Since he didn't give abortions—his job was to bring babies into the world, not speed up their leaving it—that meant another loan. And Amber already owed him plenty.

Sighing, he stood and crossed to the chair to retrieve the remote control for the television from the table. As he stooped to pick it up, he noticed the banana peel on the floor. A banana peel? Squatting down, he picked it up.

He held it between his thumb and forefinger as he straightened, a smile building as he temporarily forgot Amber's troubles. Cecile's version of breakfast, he was sure. He flopped down in the chair, lifted his hand, took careful aim and sent the peel flying. It hit the center of the wastebasket beside his desk with a damp thump.

He'd call her, he decided—Cecile, not Amber, he'd deal with that particular nightmare later—and make plans for the rest of their day. A declaration of love required a certain ambience. Candlelight, wine. He chuckled as he watched Daffy Duck flip across the television screen. Or maybe a baseball game might be more to Cecile's taste.

He settled back in his chair and thumbed the Off button on the remote control. The television screen went black and silence hummed in the room while thoughts of Cecile filled his mind as he imagined what their lives together would be like.

The phone rang, dragging him back to the present. He started to rise, but stopped when the answering machine clicked on. The sound of his own voice filled the room, then Amber's.

"Oh, Rand, I forgot to leave my new number."

His smile slowly faded. He dropped back down in the chair Cecile had sat in not long ago, his gaze frozen on the phone.

"I'm staying with a friend. The number is 555-0789. Thanks, Rand."

"Oh, God, no," he groaned, dropping his head back. The reason behind Cecile's absence was suddenly crystal clear.

She'd heard Amber's message.

* * *

Cecile unlocked the back door to the store, checked to make sure the alarm system was disengaged, then yelled, "Hey! It's me, Cecile."

Malinda appeared in the doorway leading to the front of the store, an armload of dresses hugged to her waist. "What are you doing here?" she asked in surprise. "I thought you were supposed to be spending the day with Rand?"

Cecile frowned. "Change of plans." She closed the back door and set the lock. "Did the fall shipment arrive?"

Her forehead knitted in puzzlement at her partner's unexpected appearance, Malinda replied thoughtfully, "Yes. I was just checking it in."

"Good. I'll help."

Malinda watched Cecile pace the length of the room, opening the top flaps of the boxes stacked around, then dropping them in disinterest.

"Did something happen?"

Cecile jerked up head, her frown deepening. "No, why do you ask?"

"Because you look like you could eat nails." Malinda draped the clothes she held over a box. "Did you and Rand have an argument?"

"No. As a matter of fact, he was gone when I woke up. He left a note saying he had gone to the hospital."

"And that made you angry?"

"No."

"Then what did?"

"Amber."

Malinda looked at her in confusion. "Who is Amber?"

Cecile waved away the question. "It doesn't matter." She picked up an invoice and pretended to study it. "Where do we start?"

Malinda snatched the invoice from her hand and when Cecile tried to grab it back, hid the paper behind her back. "We don't until you tell me what's going on."

Cecile gave her a dirty look, then sighed and dropped down on an unopened box. She knew Malinda wouldn't let up until she knew all the gory details. A lifelong friendship had taught her that. "I don't know exactly. But some woman named Amber called while Rand was gone and left a message saying she was pregnant and needed Rand's help."

"So? Rand's an obstetrician. Women call him all the time and tell him they think they are pregnant and need his help. What's the big deal?"

"The big deal is, he's the father."

Malinda's eyes widened in surprise. "Rand? Are you sure?"

"Yep." She pushed her hands against her knees and rose. "She said she was sorry she hadn't been more careful and that she loved him."

Malinda stared at Cecile, unable to believe what she'd just heard. "Did you ask him about it?"

Cecile frowned at her. "Why? So he could tell me some wonderfully creative lie?" She grabbed up the armload of clothes Malinda had laid down. "Let's get busy."

"But, Cecile," Malinda argued, catching her at the elbow before she could escape. "Rand's not like Denton."

"No," she replied, turning eyes bright with tears on Malinda. "He's worse."

It took Rand a while to find her. He called her house, her mother's and finally the Brannan's. Jack was the one who suggested checking at the store. Rather than call and risk her hanging up on him, he decided a personal visit might be best.

When he arrived, he saw both her car and Malinda's parked around back. He hadn't counted on Malinda being there, but quickly decided her presence might be to his advantage. Malinda was a fair-minded woman, always willing to listen to reason . . . and she liked Rand. She might serve well as a mediator if Cecile refused to listen to reason. Circling around to the back, he parked next to Cecile's Jeep and climbed from his car.

Dread knotted his stomach while he waited for someone to respond to his knock. He hadn't felt this level of apprehension since he was eleven years old and Mrs. Baxter had made him go next door and confess to cutting a bouquet of flowers from the neighbor's rose garden. The fear could be understood then, for he'd been guilty of that crime. But not this one.

He heard a movement from the opposite side of the door and squared his shoulders, preparing himself for what he knew would be a difficult confrontation. Cecile was not an easy woman to deal with even under the best of circumstances. But when the door opened, it was Malinda who stood before him. Her chin lifted when she saw him, and a distinctive coolness turned her blue eyes to ice.

So much for her being on his side.

"Is Cecile here?"

"Yes."

When she didn't call for Cecile or offer to get her for him, Rand heaved a frustrated breath. It appeared he'd already been tried and found guilty. "Well, could I please talk to her?"

"I'll ask." She turned on her heel and marched away, leaving Rand standing in the doorway.

He stepped inside and closed the door behind him. He stood waiting, listening to their muffled voices coming from the front of the store.

"Rand's here," he heard Malinda say.

"Tell him to get lost."

"At least talk to him, Cecile."

"Why? He doesn't owe me an explanation, and I certainly don't care to hear one."

So, it was true. She had heard Amber's message. And so like Cecile, she'd jumped to her own conclusion—the wrong the one. Rand had heard enough. He shoved past the boxes littering the workroom and charged toward the front of the store. "Well, you're going to hear one, anyway."

Cecile snapped up her head to glare at him, but remained silent.

"If you'll excuse me," Malinda said quietly, "there are some invoices I need to check." She glanced at Cecile and touched her arm in reassurance as she walked past. "I'll be in the office."

Cecile shifted a pile of sweaters on the counter to make room for a new stack that hadn't been priced yet. "Make it fast. I'm busy."

Rand firmed his lips, angered by her aloofness. "I assume you heard Amber's message."

"If you're referring to the woman who called to tell you she was pregnant, yes, I heard." Avoiding his gaze, she picked up a sweater and shook it out, examining it for flaws. "Although my hearing the message wasn't intentional. I was watching television."

"Yes, I know. I saw the banana peel." He took a step closer. "It's not my baby, Cecile, if that's what you're thinking."

Her hands froze for a split second, then resumed their movement. "I never said it was." She refolded the sweater and punched one of the store's price tags into the label at the sweater's neck.

"Amber's a friend."

Cecile's head snapped up, her knuckles white on the handle of the pricing gun she held. "You have a lot of those, don't you?"

Her sarcasm wasn't lost on Rand, though it angered him. He knew she was referring to Marcia and her appearance at the ball game. But he'd explained all that and thought she'd understood.

"Not really, but obviously you think I do." He took another step, this one placing him opposite her, the counter all that separated them. "They are friends, Cecile, that's all. I wish you'd believe that."

"Whether I believe you or not doesn't matter," she said, tossing the sweater aside and picking up another.

He laid his hand on hers, stilling her agitated movements and drawing her gaze to his. "It does to me."

Their gazes locked, Cecile stared at him, emotion tightening her throat and her chest. It hurt just to look at him. She wouldn't believe him, she couldn't, she told herself. She'd traveled that path before. She tore her gaze from his and turned away. She stooped to pick up a box of clothing she'd already marked. "You'll have to excuse me, Rand, but I'm really busy." Hefting the box up, she turned her back on him and walked away.

Cecile heard the pad of feet on the carpet first, then felt warm breath, scented with strawberry, against her neck. She kept her eyes closed, pretending sleep, hoping the intruder would leave her to her misery.

"Mama?"

No such luck, for when she didn't move, CeeCee only whispered louder. "Mama!"

Cecile let out a heavy sigh. "Yes, CeeCee?"

"I'm bored and the boys won't play with me."

Cecile already knew this. She'd heard the verbal battle coming from the den and chosen to ignore it. She was deeply involved in a pity party for one and hadn't the heart or the patience to act as referee. "Sorry, sweetheart. Why don't you play with your baby dolls?"

CeeCee let out a long, forlorn breath. "That's no fun by myself. Could I invite a friend over to play?"

"Fine with me. Just remember you have to pick up any messes you make."

"I promise." Strawberry-flavored lips hit Cecile's in a slobbery smack and in spite of her blue mood, Cecile smiled. She lifted her head and opened her eyes in time to catch sight of CeeCee's backside as she bounded away, lop-sided pigtails flying. With her daughter's problem resolved for the moment, she laid back down, let her eyelids drift closed and focused on her own.

Her smile quickly became a pout. How had she been suckered in by him? She, who had been fooled by the best of them, surely should have seen through Rand Coursey's innocent, boy-next-door facade. The fact that she hadn't turned her pout into a scowl.

The jerk.

And that's what he was, too. A lying, no-good, two-timing jerk! Disgusted with herself and the way she'd played right into his hands, she flounced onto her side to face the back of the sofa. She'd give herself this one afternoon to mourn what might have been—or her stupidity, whichever fit—then she was going to pull herself up by the bootstraps and forget she ever knew the jerk.

The doorbell rang as she decided this, and she pulled a pillow over her head. With three kids in the house, her duties as doorman weren't needed. When it rang the second time, she lifted her head and yelled, "CeeCee! Jenny's here, get the door!" and promptly pulled the pillow over her head again. On the third ring, she rolled to her feet, biting back a growl.

"I'm coming, I'm coming. Keep your pants on," she said irritably as she staggered to the door. She jerked it open, already giving instructions, "CeeCee's probably in her room waiting—"

The rest of the statement died on her lips when her gaze landed on a belt buckle instead of Jenny's carrot-colored hair. Swallowing hard, she lifted her gaze, passing over a carefully pressed denim shirt, a cleft chin, and a familiar set of lips. Her eyes leveled on a pair of brown eyes. It was an effort, but she put steel in her veins.

"Take a hint, Coursey, I don't want to talk to you." She gave the door a shove, but Rand slapped a hand against it before it slammed in his face.

He took a step inside and pushed the door closed behind him. "I didn't come to talk to you, I came to see CeeCee."

"CeeCee?" she parroted.

"Yes, CeeCee. She called and ask me to come over and play."

Cecile's mouth fell open. "And you agreed?"

"Certainly. Is there a problem?"

"Yes! No!" Cecile sank her fingers into her hair and tried not to scream. Fighting for control, she wheeled away from him and dropped her hands to her sides. She let a good five seconds hum by before she turned to face him. "Look. I know why you're here, and it won't work. Okay? Our relationship is over. *Finis. Nada.* The end. Understand?"

"Perfectly."

"Then why are you here?"

"CeeCee called and asked me—"

"You said that already."

"Yes, I believe I did."

Cecile tightened her lips. "And I'm supposed to believe that's why you're here?"

"You can believe whatever you like." He looked down his nose at her, arching one brow slightly. "I've found you usually do."

The accusation in his tone was like a knife in Cecile's heart. But she was right—she knew she was—in ending her relationship with him. Continuing would only result in more heartbreak, and she didn't think she could stand that.

Rand saw the distress in her eyes and felt a stab of guilt. "I'm sorry, Cecile. That was uncalled for."

"No harm done." She forced a smile. "CeeCee's in her room. I'll get her." Anxious to get away from him, she turned.

Rand caught her arm before she could escape. She tensed at his touch and whirled. Rand softened his grip and let his hand slide down the length of her arm to catch her hand in his. The effect was like being struck by lightning. "I thought we agreed to be friends."

"Did we?"

"Yes, we did," he said, tightening his fingers on hers. "I hope you'll honor that promise."

Her eyes riveted to his, Cecile backed away, dragging her hand from his. "Yeah, whatever you say. I'll get CeeCee." She turned and walked away, careful to keep her footsteps slow and deliberate even though she felt like tearing down the hall in a flat-out run.

Ten

Rand shrugged out of his white smock, then carefully draped it over the back of his chair before sitting down at his desk. In front of him were three stacks, the first being a neat pile of patient records to be reviewed for the next morning's appointments, the second, correspondence that required his signature, and the third, phone messages he needed to return.

He loved the order, the routine of his efficiently run office. Today, he was thankful for it.

As was his habit, he reached for the phone messages first to place them in a prioritized sequence. He kept his hands steady, his pace purposely slow, though with each flip of a page he prayed he'd see Cecile's name with a request for him to call.

The first sheet recorded a call from an associate, Ben Truman, thanking him for a referral. A flip of the hand and Marjorie Stewart's name appeared with a request for him to speak at a local women's club, topic: childbirth in the 90s. He thumbed through the list, setting aside those that required a response but stopped when he came to the name Joey Barker. His receptionist had written that the call arrived at 4:45. Emergency was written in bold print. He glanced at his wristwatch and was surprised to see that it was almost eight.

Joey Barker. Rand tapped the corner of the memo against the side of his thumb, trying to place the name. To his knowledge he didn't have a patient by the name of Barker. He looked at the message again. *Emergency.*

His stomach clenched and his fingers tightened on the memo. Joey. He reached for the phone, quickly punching in Cecile's number.

"Hello?"

"Cecile. It's Rand. Is Joey's last name Barker?"

There was a long pause. Fearing she would hang up, he demanded, "Well, is it?"

"Yes. Why?"

"I have a phone message to call him. Says it's an emergency. Hold on a minute." He quickly pushed a button placing Cecile on hold, then punched in the telephone number recorded on the memo. A busy signal buzzed in his ear.

By the time he clicked back to Cecile, a fine sheen of perspiration had broken out on his forehead. "The line's busy. I'm going over there."

"I'm going with you."

"That's not necess—"

"Fine, then I'll meet you there." The line went dead before he could argue the point. "Damn!" He shoved his chair back and stood. He didn't want Cecile there. He didn't know what kind of emergency this was, but if it was what he expected, he wanted desperately to spare Cecile witnessing firsthand the damage arms like Popeye's could do to a small child. From personal experience, he knew it wasn't a pretty sight.

Ten minutes later Rand was pulling up in front of Joey's house. Cecile's Jeep was parked at the curb. Thankfully, she was still sitting behind the wheel. Rand jumped from his car, but she had her door open and was stepping out by the time he reached her. The glint in her eyes and the defiant lift of her chin told him she wasn't leaving.

He planted his hands on her shoulders, forcing her to look at him. "Go home, Cecile. I'll handle this."

"Fine. Handle it, but I'm still going with you."

She pushed past him, headed for the front door. Rand caught up with her in two steps, catching her by the elbow and yanking her to a halt.

"Listen, Cecile. We don't know what's happened. Hopefully, nothing. But if the boyfriend's been using Joey as a punching bag and the guy's still around, I don't want you anywhere near the place."

Cecile jerked her elbow from his grasp. "Tough. Now do you ring the doorbell or do I?"

The defiant set of her chin told Rand he was wasting his time arguing with her. Catching her by the elbow, he guided her toward the porch. "I do. But if there's trouble, I want you to run like hell and call the police. Understand?"

"Yes, sir."

Rand ignored the sarcasm in her reply. He punched the doorbell and waited. Seconds passed without a sound from inside. He punched it again, then lifted his fist to the door and pounded.

A female voice called from inside, "Who's there?"

"It's Cecile Kingsley, Joanne," Cecile blurted out before Rand could speak. "Can I talk to you?"

"I'm not dressed." There was a slight hesitation in which Cecile held her breath before the woman added, "Can you give me a minute?"

Cecile's breath sagged out of her. "Sure."

"I said I'd handle it," Rand muttered.

"She's a woman, probably scared out of her wits and doesn't know you from Adam. Now who do you think she would open the door for, Rand Coursey or Cecile Kingsley?"

Seeing the wisdom in her argument but refusing to acknowledge it, Rand folded his arms across his chest and waited.

Less than five minutes passed before the lock clicked and the door creaked open a crack, but it seemed like an eternity to the two waiting on the front porch. A petite woman, in Rand's estimation too young to have a son Joey's age, peeked through the opening. Her bleached blond hair was disheveled, and she lifted a hand to comb at it as her eyes darted nervously from Cecile to Rand and back again.

She clutched the V opening of the wrapper she'd tossed on over her breasts. "I'm sorry to keep you waiting, Cecile. What did you need?"

"Joey called. He said it was an emergency."

Joanne's eyes widened in surprise before she caught herself. She forced a laugh. "You know how little boys are. Always into trouble. Making prank calls again. I'll have a talk with him. Sorry he bothered you."

She started to close the door, but Rand stuck a foot in the opening before she could lock them out. "We'd like to talk to him."

"Well—" She glanced over her shoulder, her fingers nervously working the top button at the wrapper's V. "He's asleep right now, and I hate to wake him."

Though he felt like ramming a hand through a wall, Rand made his voice remain calm. "It's important."

"I'll have him call you tomorrow." Again she pushed at the door, but Rand flattened a hand against it.

"We're not leaving until we see Joey."

Tears budded in the woman's eyes and her lips began to tremble. "I didn't do it, I swear. Dave did. He didn't mean to hurt Joey, I know he didn't. But he'd been drinking, and Joey smarted off to him."

Rand shoved the door, knocking Joanne back a step. He pushed by her, intent on finding Joey. Joanne hurried to keep up with him. "I tried to tell Joey. I told him if he'd just keep his mouth shut, Dave wouldn't have no reason to hit him. But he wouldn't listen. And now—" She pressed her hands to her mouth when Rand reached Joey's door. She hung back when Rand shoved it open.

The room looked like a cyclone had blown through . . . or a war had been fought. Books, toys and clothes were scattered about the floor and a mirror hung cockeyed over a scarred dresser.

"Joey?" Rand took a cautious step inside, his gaze shifting left and right, without seeing any sign of the boy. "Joey, it's me, Rand Coursey. Are you in here?"

The closet door on Rand's left squeaked open. Five heart-stopping seconds ticked by before Joey stepped out, his chin tucked against his chest.

"Joey?" Rand took a step toward him. "Are you okay?"

Slowly the boy lifted his head, and Rand felt his heart twist in his chest. Cecile's gasp behind him let him know that she had followed him into the room and that she, too, had seen the damage that arms like Popeye's could do to a small child.

Rand crossed to the boy and dropped to a knee in front of him. "Joey. Oh, Joey," he murmured sadly, and pulled the boy into his arms. The boy remained stiff, refusing to let go of the emotions Rand knew must be bottled up inside. "It's okay, Joey," he whispered against the boy's ear as he held him. "I'm here and I'm going to take care of you."

A shudder passed through the boy, then Rand felt hot tears wet his shirt front where the boy hid his face. Clutching the child tighter, he soothed, "It's okay, Joey. Cry all you want. Nobody's going to hurt you ever again. You have my word on it."

Rand sat at the kitchen table while Joanne scurried about, making coffee. He'd purposefully delegated Cecile to help Joey put his room back in order so he could be alone with the boy's mother.

"You're sure he's okay?" Joanne asked for the nineteenth time.

"Yes, as far as I can determine. But I'd like for you to take him for X rays in the morning, just to be on the safe side." He patted the table. "Sit down, Joanne. We need to talk."

Her hand shook as she scooted a cup of coffee in front of Rand. She sat opposite him, nervously twisting her hands in the folds of her wrapper. "I'm not a bad mother, Dr. Coursey."

"I never said you were, Joanne." He took a deep breath, searching for just the right words. "But you have some choices to make."

Fear darkened her eyes. "You won't take him away from me, will you? Joey's just a baby, he's all I've got."

Rand laid a hand on her fisted hands in an effort to reassure her. "No, Joanne. It's not my place to take Joey away. But he needs a home. A safe one. If you can't provide that for him, then maybe you should consider placing him with someone who can. Do you have family?"

Her head moved frantically from side to side. "No. No one." She lifted shaking fingers to wipe a tear from her cheek. "It's just Joey and me."

A loud thump from outside had her jumping to her feet, her eyes wide in fear. Rand crossed to the kitchen window and peered out. A cat, silhouetted by the moon, walked the back fence.

"It's just a cat," he said as he guided Joanne back to the chair. "Are you afraid of Dave?"

"Only when he's drinking," she replied, her eyes darting nervously to the back door. "When he's sober, he's really a nice guy."

Rand knew the type. The second time around, his own mother had married one.

While he watched, Joanne glanced around the room, her fingers knotting and unknotting in her lap. "Without Dave, I don't know what I'd do. He helps with the rent and the bills." Fresh tears budded and brimmed over red-rimmed eyes. "I know you probably think I'm crazy, but I love Dave, Dr. Coursey. I really do."

The feeling was fairly new for him, but Rand understood love and the pain associated with it, and knew, too, that it wasn't an emotion you could pick and choose. "I'm sure you do," he said, his own heart heavy with loss. "But Dave needs help, and until he gets it, you and Joey aren't safe. There are shelters where you could go. Places where you and Joey would be cared for and maybe Dave could receive the help he needs. Why don't you let me make a few calls, see what's available? Then you and Joey can go and check the place out. What do you say?"

Her fingers continued their nervous twisting. "But what about Dave? What if he gets mad and refuses to get help?" Her lips parted, her eyes widening as a new fear took hold. "Oh, God, what if he leaves me?"

Though it was his nature to comfort, Rand made himself remain in his chair. "That's a chance you'll have to be willing to take. The alternative is to lose Joey. The choice isn't an easy one, but it's yours to make."

He waited, silently willing her to make the right decision while she stared at him, her eyes wide in fear.

Finally she stood, her hands hugged tight at her waist, her eyes bright with tears. "Make your calls, Dr. Coursey. I'll pack me and Joey a bag."

The ride back to Joey's house from the shelter Cecile and Rand had delivered him and his mother to was the longest ride in her life. Cecile felt brittle, as if at the slightest touch she'd shatter into a million pieces.

The memory of the look on Joey's face when they'd left wouldn't go away. He had stood in the drab lobby of the shelter, his hand squeezed tight around his mother's watching as she and Rand had driven away. His face was distorted by swelling and vivid with the color of bruising, yet he stood at his mother's side with his hand locked tightly around hers as if he were the adult protecting her.

And he was just a baby. Oh, she knew he'd hate it if he knew she considered him such, but dammit, he was a baby. Only ten years old, but already wise beyond his years. She fought back a shudder, digging her fingers into the door's armrest. She wouldn't cry. Not yet, anyway. If she did, she feared she'd never be able to stop.

She let out a ragged breath when Rand pulled up behind her Jeep. Without a word to him, she bolted from his car anxious to reach the privacy of her own before she broke down. When she rounded the hood of Rand's car, tears already blinded her eyes.

"Cecile?"

She slammed against him before she could stop. "I've got to get home," she murmured as she tried to brush past him.

He sidestepped, blocking her path. "No, wait. Please."

She lifted her gaze. The streetlight on the corner illuminated her face. The tears were there, but banked, leaving her face ravaged by an anguish that ripped like a knife through Rand's chest. He opened his arms.

Cecile fell into them on a strangled sob. "Oh, my God, Rand. Did you see his face? The poor little baby. How could anyone be so mean, so vile?"

"I know, Cecile," he soothed, tucking her head beneath his chin. He cradled her head in the width of his hand and let out a sigh as her tears wet the front of his shirt still damp from Joey's tears. "I know."

She sobbed uncontrollably, her fingers clawing at his shirt. Suddenly she pushed away, angrily dragging her palms beneath her eyes. "I'd like to get my hands on that miserable son of a bitch. I'd—"

Rand pulled her back against his chest, pinning her arms between them. "Hush, now. You don't mean that."

"But I do," she cried against his chest as another sob shook her slim shoulders. Rand hugged her tighter, trying to absorb her pain.

"I know, Cecile. But revenge won't help Joey. We've done all we can do. I only hope his mother has the courage to stand her ground."

"If she doesn't, and that man lays a hand on Joey, I swear I'll make him wish he'd never been born."

Rand smiled against her hair at her tough talk. "I'm sure you will." He placed a finger beneath her chin to tip her face up to his. "I hear you're pretty good at chasing off monsters."

His comment produced the desired result, for a watery smile trembled at her lips. She sighed as she looked up at him, then touched a hand to his cheek. "Joey Barker is a very lucky young man to have a friend like you."

The tenderness in the gesture twisted violently in Rand's chest. He reached up to cover her hand with his. "Or like you." The pain was only a shadow in her eyes now, and her mouth only a breath away. Rand closed the distance and touched his lips to hers. She accepted him on a sigh.

In the touch of his lips, Cecile found the comfort she needed, the strength to wash away her fears. Giving in to it, she parted her lips on a moan.

"I love you, Cecile," he murmured against her lips, his hands tightening around her. "And I've missed you so much."

She stiffened in his arms. No, she cried inwardly. He doesn't love me. They're just words. Hurtful words. She twisted from his arms, her breath hitching in her lungs as she looked up at him. She saw the surprise in his eyes, but more the passion . . . and hated him for it.

She covered her face with her hands, blocking out his image. She whirled, blinded by tears, and ran for the safety of her Jeep.

"He doesn't play fair." Cecile took Madison from the portable swing and settled her in her lap as she sank down on Malinda's bed.

Malinda looked up from the change table where she was diapering Lila. "Joey or Rand?"

Cecile rolled her eyes. "Rand. Are you paying attention to anything I'm saying?"

"Yes, but you keep flipping from topic to topic so quickly, I'm having a hard time keeping up. So how's Rand not being fair?"

"He's being a friend."

Malinda snorted and returned to her diapering. "Oh, that's unfair, all right."

"No, you don't understand. He knew I was upset about Joey and he used my emotional state to play up to me."

"He might have been just offering comfort."

"Maybe," Cecile replied doubtfully. "But he certainly didn't need to kiss me."

Malinda looked back over her shoulder. "He kissed you?"

"Yeah."

"And did you kiss him back?"

Cecile caught her lower lip between her teeth, a sure sign of guilt. Malinda bit back a smile as she turned back to Lila. "I'm sure he didn't mean anything by it."

"Oh, but that's not all," Cecile exclaimed, anxious to prove her point. "He's driving me crazy! He drops by unexpectedly. Brings little gifts for CeeCee. He even took Gordy to the Omniplex to see some special science fair display." Enchanted by Madison's cherubic cheeks, she paused long enough to feather a kiss on each one. "Now Gordy wants to be a doctor, just like Rand."

"What a nightmare," Malinda replied, cutting her eyes to Cecile.

"Well, it is," Cecile said defensively. "After all, the man got a woman pregnant. He should be spending his time at *her* house, not mine."

Malinda shook her head as she ripped the adhesive gaurd from the diaper and pressed it in place. "Rand getting a woman pregnant. I mean—well, heavens! He's an obstetrician, for pity's sake. If anyone should be aware of birth control, it would be him. And besides," she said, shaking her head, unable to believe any of the things Cecile had told her were true. "He simply isn't the kind to sleep around, and he hasn't mentioned anything to Jack or me about having a woman in his life." She picked up Lila and nuzzled the baby's cheek to hers as she moved to join Cecile on the bed.

Cecile scooted over, giving her room to sit down. "Did he tell you he was sleeping with me?"

"Well, no. But—"

"I rest my case."

Malinda pursed her lips and narrowed an eye at her. "As I was about to say before I was so rudely interrupted, he didn't have to. It was obvious. Besides, I know Rand cares about you."

Cecile tipped back her head and laughed. "Yeah, the man's a great actor, all right."

"It's no act. Rand genuinely cares about you."

"Oh, and how do you know that?"

Malinda lifted her chin. "I just know."

Cecile chuckled as she leaned to tickle Madison under her chin. "Your mother thinks she's pretty smart, Madison. But this time, she's wrong. Dead wrong."

"Is this a hen party, or can I come in?"

Malinda and Cecile both lifted their heads to find Jack standing in the doorway. Mortified that he might have heard any of their conversation, Cecile simply stared.

Malinda rose, crossed to Jack and plunked Lila in his arms. "Yes, it's a hen party and, yes, you can come in." She rose to her toes, lifting her face for a kiss. She patted his cheek as she lowered her heels to the floor, thankful for his presence in her life and the fact that she no longer had to deal with the trials and tribulations of the dating game.

"Do you know a friend of Rand's by the name of Amber?" she asked as she looped her arm through Jack's, ignoring Cecile's shocked intake of breath.

"Lord, is she still around?" He shook his head as he settled Lila next to Madison on the bed, then dropped down beside them. "Yeah, I know her, though I'm not proud of the fact."

Cecile shot Malinda a look that had "I told you so" written all over it before she turned her attention back to Jack, smiling smugly as she listened to her husband's explanation.

"She was one of the foster kids at the Baxters's house. Wild as a March hare and lazy as a hound. She had just hit the teenage years when I moved out." He kicked off his shoes and leaned back on his elbows, warming to the story. "She was in trouble all the time. At school, with the police." He shook his head, chuckling. "For some reason, Rand took pity on the kid and believe you me, she milked him for all he was worth. He was all the time covering for her, doing her chores, helping her with her homework, pleading her case to the Baxters. Hell, if it hadn't been for Rand, she'd have ended up in juvenile hall before she was sixteen." Lila fussed, and he leaned to pop her pacifier in her mouth.

Cecile watched him, swallowing back the wad of guilt threatening to choke her.

"So she isn't a girlfriend of Rand's?" Malinda asked quietly.

Jack whipped his head around to stare at his wife in surprise. "Girlfriend," he echoed, then tossed back his head and laughed. "A leech maybe, but not a girlfriend."

Cecile felt the heat of Malinda's gaze and finally found the courage to look at her. Malinda stood at Jack's feet, her arms folded at her waist, her chin tucked to her chest, her eyes narrowed on Cecile.

Cecile tried to smile, but it melted under Malinda's censorious gaze. Frowning, she lifted a hand and let it drop. "Well, how was I to know?" she muttered defensively.

Eleven

"I'm sorry."

Cecile let the words roll slowly off her tongue, testing, tasting and weighing. She made a gagging sound as she shoved a load of towels into the dryer.

Even though the words were sincere and heartfelt, they still left a bitter taste in her mouth. Apologies never came easy for her, and this one was even more difficult for the wrong was all hers and the apology long overdue.

Four days she'd stewed. Four days of mentally beating herself up for not being more trusting of Rand, more willing to listen to his explanation. She'd been a fool. A stubborn, mule-headed fool. Nothing new, she thought ruefully, but this time her stubbornness may have cost her more than she was prepared to lose. She'd call him, she decided, and tell him she was sorry.

A whining sound behind her made her grimace. "Hold your horses, Shaggy," she mumbled as she slammed the dryer door and punched the Start button. Though she tried hard to hide her affection for the dog, she spoiled him as much as CeeCee. She gave the dog a rub behind the ears before opening the door and watching him slink through the opening. The fact that the dog's sides rubbed as he passed through the doorway didn't pass Cecile's notice. She made a mental note to double check the portions CeeCee was feeding him as she shut the door behind him. The dog looked as fat as a tick!

From the den the canned sounds of a Nintendo video game and an occasional frustrated grunt or a cheer told her the kids for the moment were occupied. She tiptoed from the laundry room through the kitchen and slipped down the hall to her bedroom. It wouldn't do for the kids to hear if she were forced to grovel when she offered the apology. They'd never let her live it down.

She hadn't expected nervousness, but it was there, dampening her palms, trembling at her fingers. Tightening her grip on the receiver, she sank to the bed and punched in his home number. She forced herself to take slow, deep breaths while she waited through three rings. Then his voice came through the line.

"Hello. You have reached the residence of Dr. Rand Coursey." Her shoulders sagged and her heart plummeted at the recorded voice. "I'm unable to answer your call at the moment, but you may leave a message after the tone and I'll return your call as soon as possible. If this is an emergency, you may call my service at 555-2875."

Though tempted to take the coward's way out and leave her apology on his machine, Cecile punched the plunger, breaking the connection. As much as she dreaded the confrontation, he deserved to hear her apology in person. She gnawed her lower lip a moment, trying to decide if she should call his service and leave a message. Replacing the receiver, she shook her head. No, he'd said to call his service if it was an emergency. And though she herself felt impending doom, she knew her apology didn't fall into the emergency category.

Her cheeks puffed on a weary exhalation of breath as she levered herself from the bed. She'd try again, she assured herself. And again. And again. Even if it took all night. She winced after making the rash promise and sent up a fervent prayer that Rand wouldn't be caught at the hospital all night delivering babies. She didn't think her growing ulcer would bear the wait.

Gathering a pile of dirty clothes from the floor, she headed for the bedroom door. She stopped, listening, when she heard a noise outside her French doors. Straining, she crossed to the door and thought she detected the sound of a low whine.

"That dang dog," she muttered irritably as she let the towels drop to the carpet. CeeCee probably fed him another candy bar and now he's sick. At least this time he'd had the good sense to seek outdoors instead of the entry hall Oriental rug he'd chosen for his last bout of nausea.

She opened the door. "Shaggy?" She listened as she glanced around the empty patio. A scattering of mulch and dirt on the pebbled concrete had her lips thinning. "A digger," she muttered her breath. "And if he thinks he's going to dig up all my plants, he's got another think coming." She marched across the patio and stooped, pushing aside the shrubs to peer inside. Sure enough, there lay Shaggy, tongue lolling, sides heaving, lying in a freshly dug hole. "Out, Shaggy," she ordered angrily. When he continued to lie there, staring at her, she reached inside to grab hold of his collar and haul him out.

A low growl and a set of bared teeth had her rocking back on her heels. She snatched her hand from among the tangled shrubs and hid it behind her back. After a moment she found the courage to peek through the thick barrier of leaves. What she saw made her mouth drop open. "Oh, my stars," she whispered as she gently pushed more of the branches aside to gain a better look at the puppy pushing its way into the world. "And all this time we thought you were a boy."

A tiny whimper coming from farther down the flower bed had her spinning on her heels. Dropping the shrubs back in place, she crawled along the edge of the patio, listening. When she heard the sound again, she pushed back the shrubs to find another hole and a small lump with dirt scattered over its top.

"Dear, God!" she exclaimed as she scrambled to her feet. "That fool dog is burying her puppies." She ran into the house, grabbed a handful of towels from the floor where she'd dropped them earlier and ran back outside. Kneeling, she gathered the puppy into a towel and began to brush the dirt from it using the soft, terry fabric.

A rustling sound had her looking over her shoulder. Shaggy was standing at the edge of the patio, frantically pawing dirt into the hole where she'd just given birth.

"Shaggy! Stop!" she screamed. "Dent! Gordy! Come quick!" Cradling the puppy to her waist, she rushed over and grabbed a hold of Shaggy's collar, ignoring the low growl rumbling low in the dog's throat.

The door crashed open behind her and CeeCee burst out. "What's wrong, Mama?"

"Shaggy's having puppies. Tell Dent to call the doctor."

CeeCee surged forward, her eyes wide in wonder. "Really? Where are they?"

Cecile latched on to her daughter's arm before she could slip by her. "CeeCee! Listen carefully and do as I say. Now go and get Dent and tell him to call the doctor. When he has him on the phone, tell him to bring me the portable.''

CeeCee backed toward the door, her gaze locked on Shaggy. When her bottom bumped the French door, she whirled and bolted through screaming, ''Dent! Gordy! Come quick! Shaggy's having babies!''

Within seconds both boys were at Cecile's side. She shoved the puppy she held to Gordy. ''Here. Keep this one wrapped up and warm.'' She crawled toward the newest grave, the pebbles on the patio chewing at her bare knees. ''Where's the phone?'' she tossed back over her shoulder.

''CeeCee's bringing it.''

Swallowing back her fear, Cecile gently scraped away the dirt. Dent shoved a towel at her and she used it to wrap the puppy as she eased it into her hands. Quickly she cleaned the worst of the dirt away and rubbed, all the while watching for signs of life. When she saw the puppy's sides swell, she breathed a sigh of relief.

Her relief disappeared when she glanced around, looking for Shaggy. The dog was nowhere in sight. She couldn't see her, but she could hear the low moans coming from deep within the shrubbery.

At that moment CeeCee ran out and pushed the portable phone beneath Cecile's nose. ''Here, Mama!'' She took the bundle Cecile pushed at her, exchanging it for the phone.

''Doc, I need your help,'' Cecile gasped. ''Our dog is having puppies.''

''Shaggy?''

At the sound of Rand's voice, Cecile's mouth fell open and she slowly turned her head to glare at CeeCee. She slapped a hand over the mouthpiece. ''I thought I told you to call the vet.''

''You said call the doctor.''

Cecile rolled her eyes.

"Cecile? Are you there?"

Cecile dropped her hand from the mouthpiece and shoved hard at her bangs. "Yes, I'm here."

"Is there a problem?"

Unwanted tears welled in Cecile's eyes. "Yes, there's a problem," she snapped, her voice rising hysterically. "Shaggy's burying the puppies as fast as they hit the ground."

"You need to calm her down."

"Calm *her* down?" she screeched. "Who's going to calm *me* down? I've only got two hands and this stupid dog is burying puppies faster than I can dig them up."

"Move her to the garage. She can't dig on concrete."

Cecile looked up as Shaggy crawled from beneath the shrubs. "Okay. Then what?"

"I'll get there as fast as I can."

"No, you don't need to—" but she was talking to a dial tone. Stifling a groan, she slapped a palm to the antenna and tossed the portable to the patio. Taking a deep breath, she squared her shoulders. "Okay, kids. Here's the plan. Gordy, you and CeeCee go open the garage door. Take the puppies with you. Dent," she said, looking at her oldest. "You're going to have to help me get Shaggy to the garage." The look on her son's face told her he didn't relish this task any more than she did.

Softening her tone to a cajoling one, she turned to the dog. "Come on, Shaggy. Come on, girl. We're going to make you a nice bed in the garage."

Though Rand had made it sound simple enough, it took both Cecile and Dent a good ten minutes to half drag, half push the reluctant dog to the garage. Once inside, Cecile closed the garage door and quickly started making a bed out of a tattered lounge chair cushion and an old quilt. Shaggy paced around the makeshift bed, sniffing and whimpering.

As soon as Cecile stepped away, Shaggy flopped down and immediately began to deliver a third pup.

Dent, Gordy and CeeCee stood silently by, watching, their eyes wide. As far as sex education went, Cecile figured this was as good a way as any to learn. Her children's comments ranged from "Wow" to "Yuck" while they watched two more pups enter the world.

"How's the mother doing?"

Cecile twisted to find Rand standing just behind her. She'd been so enthralled at the scene being enacted in front of her, she hadn't even heard him arrive. As usual, his presence brought comfort. "I'm better, thanks."

Rand chuckled. "No, I meant Shaggy. How's she doing?"

Heat flooded Cecile's face and she turned away. "She's better, too. Or at least, I think she is," she said, a frown furrowing her brow. "She's had four, so far. How do you know when she's through?"

"Beats me."

Cecile snapped her head around, then scowled when she saw the teasing glint in his eye. "Funny, Coursey. Very funny."

He shrugged out of his sport coat and draped it over the handles of the lawnmower, then began rolling up his sleeves. "Let's have a look."

Much to Cecile's dismay, the labor lasted more than two hours. When the kids learned they wouldn't be able to play with the pups, they soon grew bored with the novelty of watching and returned to the den and their game of Nintendo.

Rand remained at her side, though, a vision of calmness. Cecile despised him for that. Personally, she was a wreck. And she couldn't blame Shaggy for her present state.

The bundle of nerves bunched in her neck and the burning sensation in her stomach were all due to Rand's presence and the apology that remained tightly lodged in her throat. Now that Rand was there and her decision to offer an apology more than a good intention, she was having a hard time forming the words.

"I'm sorry," she finally blurted out, then stretched to help a puppy find his mother's tit.

Rand cocked his head to look at her. "What?"

"I said, I'm sorry," she repeated sullenly, drawing back her hands to squeeze them between her knees.

Rand frowned at her. "It was no problem coming over, Cecile. I assure you."

She tipped back her head and groaned at the ceiling. He was going to make her say it all, the whole dang thing. "I'm not apologizing for calling you over. I'm apologizing for—well, you know . . . for the Amber thing, not trusting you."

"Oh, that."

"Yes, that. Jack told me the whole story."

Rand waited, silently watching her.

"He told me she was a foster sister and one who played on your goodness and generosity."

When he didn't say anything and continued to stare at her, Cecile scowled. "Well, aren't you going to say anything?"

"Like what?"

"Like I told you so, or that's okay, Cecile, it was an honest mistake?"

"No, I don't think either of those statements are appropriate." Shaggy emitted a low moan, and Rand shifted to lay a broad hand on her head, offering both comfort and sympathy. The dog craned her head back and licked at his hand. The thought was ridiculous, but Cecile felt like doing much the same thing. "I think she's about done," Rand said softly after checking her progress. "She's passing the afterbirth now."

Cecile curled her nose and looked away, thankful the kids had missed this portion of the birth process. Education was one thing, grossness quite another.

Since Shaggy appeared to have calmed down and was handling things on her own, Cecile rose, brushing her hair back from her face. "Come on in. I'll throw together sandwiches or something."

Rand picked up his coat and slung it over his shoulder, holding it by the tip of his index finger.

"You're inviting me in?"

Puzzled, Cecile frowned at him. "Well, certainly. Why not?"

Rand shrugged. "I'm just surprised, is all. The last couple of times I was here, you seemed to resent my presence."

Cecile had the grace to be embarrassed. "Well, that was because I didn't know." She looked at her feet, then tipped her head up and grinned. She sidled up to him and laced her arm through his. "But now that I know who Amber is and that the baby is not yours—" She angled her body until she faced him, her breasts brushing against his chest. Electricity arced between them. Her gaze riveted on his chest, she placed a finger on a button and toyed with it while a sultry smile played at the corners of her mouth. "Well, that places everything in a different light."

"It does?"

The anger in his tone, though suppressed, had her lifting her gaze.

"Sure it does," she said, a knot of fear forming in her stomach. "With that little misunderstanding out of the way, I thought—" The words backed up in her throat at the dark anger that burned in his eyes.

"You thought what, Cecile? That by offering an apology we could pick up where we left off? Lovers. That's what we were, right? Nothing more." His hands found her elbows and clamped around them like a vise. "But what about the next time, Cecile? What then? What happens when another woman leaves a message on my machine or gives me a friendly hug? Are we going to go through this all over again? Will you trust me when I tell you she's only a friend?"

Cecile stood wide-eyed, staring, unable to respond to the anger in his tone, the accusations.

Rand jerked his hands from her and turned away in disgust. "Never mind."

Cecile gave the covers tangling her feet a good kick, then jackknifed to a sitting position, her hands fisted on her knees. "Of all the nerve," she muttered, glaring at the far wall. "I apologized. What more does the man want?"

Obviously the shadows dancing on the wall didn't have an answer, either, for none was forthcoming. Cecile deepened her frown, slowly replaying their conversation over and over through her mind, trying to figure out what she'd said that had angered him so.

Frustrated and knowing that Rand was the only one who could resolve the questions keeping her awake, she swung her legs from the bed. She scooped her shorts from the floor and tugged them on. Her breasts bobbed unrestrained beneath her T-shirt. Barefoot, she marched down the hall to Dent's room.

"Dent?" She shook his shoulder until he rolled over, rubbing his eyes sleepily.

"What's wrong, Mom?" he mumbled, hitching himself up on one elbow.

"Nothing." She paced to the end of his bed and back, nervously lacing and unlacing her fingers. "I'm going to, uh, run an errand and I'm leaving you in charge."

Dent cut a glance to his bedroom window and the darkness beyond. "An errand? What time is it?"

"A little past three."

Dent flopped back against his pillow. "An errand at three o'clock in the morning? Jeez, Mom. Are you crazy?"

"No. Now listen, I'll leave a number on the refrigerator where I can be reached." She peered down at her son's face and saw that his eyes were closed. "You are awake, aren't you?"

"Yeah, I'm awake," he muttered as he rolled to pull a pillow over his head.

"And you'll call if you need me?"

"Yeah, I'll call."

Just to be sure he was fully conscious and would remember her instructions, she leaned over and picked up a corner of the pillow. "And where will the number be posted?"

"On the refrigerator," came his muffled reply.

Satisfied, Cecile dropped the pillow back in place.

Dent waited until he heard the back door close, then listened for the rev of the Jeep's engine. When he was sure Cecile was gone, he rolled to his feet and padded down the hallway to the kitchen. In the illumination of the back porch light shining through the window, he read his mother's scribbled message, "At Rand's, 555-7869. Call if you need me. Mom."

He hit a doubled fist against the note. "Damn!" He glanced quickly around to make sure no one had heard the swear word. Relieved to find himself alone, he repeated the word, though in a whisper this time. "Damn." He whipped open the refrigerator door. As long as he was awake and his life was about to be ruined, he figured he might as well have a little snack.

"I'm gonna tell."

Dent jumped, bumping his head against the edge of the freezer door. He pulled his head out of the refrigerator and turned, a dark scowl on his face. "What are you doing out of bed, CeeCee?"

"I heard a noise. I'm gonna tell," she repeated, setting her chin at a pious tilt.

"Tell what?"

"I heard you swear."

"So? You'd swear, too, if you'd just lost your most prized possession."

CeeCee's mouth puckered in disapproval. "You and Gordy've been bettin' again, haven't you?"

"Yeah, we have." The admission obviously pained him.

"What'd you bet this time?"

"My Nolan Ryan baseball card collection against his microscope that Mom and Rand wouldn't make up for another week."

Her eyes wide, CeeCee padded across the kitchen floor. "They made up?"

Dent tossed a hand over his shoulder, pointing at the note. "She's at Rand's as we speak."

A slow smile built on CeeCee's face. "She is?"

"Yeah. Which means I lost the bet." He stuck his head in the refrigerator again and came out with a plateful of pizza. "You'd think she could have waited till the weekend, wouldn't you?" He shook his head woefully as he headed for the table. "I hope he sends her packing."

CeeCee's eyes widened in alarm. "I thought you liked Rand?"

Dent shoved a bite of pizza in his mouth. "I do," he said around the mouthful. "He's pretty cool."

"Then why do you hope he sends her packing?"

"'Cause if he does and Gordy never hears about Mom going over there," he said, with a threatening look Cee-Cee's way, "then I might still win the bet."

The thought of Rand and her mother not making up made CeeCee's lower lip quiver. "But I want them to make up. I like Rand."

Dent shoved the plate of pizza her way. "Don't worry, brat. They'll make up. The two were made for each other."

CeeCee picked up a wedge, then licked the tomato sauce daintily from her fingertips as she slowly nodded her agreement. She looked at Dent over her eyelashes and smiled sweetly. "I'm still gonna tell."

Ordinarily, at three-thirty in the morning, the doorbell would have awakened Rand, but on this particular night he was already awake. After supervising the birth of Shaggy's puppies and the frustrating conversation with Cecile, he'd driven home, showered, then crawled beneath the covers and waited for sleep.

Unfortunately, sleep hadn't come.

As the doorbell continued its impatient ringing, he made his way through the darkened house to the front door. A suspicion, something formed deep in his gut, told him who he would find on the other side.

He almost smiled when he opened the door and found Cecile on his stoop, but choked instead when Cecile's fist hit him just about an inch above his navel.

"Okay, Coursey," she growled as she pushed past him. "What do you want?" She slammed the door, then stood over his stooped form while he tried to find his breath, her hands on her hips. "Groveling? Would it make you feel better if I crawled and begged?"

With a huff of breath, she whirled away. Three steps and she whirled back. "Okay!" she said, throwing her hands up in the air. "I'm sorry. Damn sorry that I didn't trust you, and sorrier still that I wouldn't listen to your explanation."

Rand slowly straightened, a palm pressed against his midsection. He was breathing again, but his eyes burned with a mixture of anger and wariness. He'd be ready this time if she decided to throw another punch.

But to his amazement, Cecile dropped to her knees and crawled to kneel at his feet, her palms flattened against each other in contrition. "I'm begging for your forgiveness. Okay? Does that make you happy? Is this what you want?"

Rand looked down at her, his stance stiff and unyielding. "No, not even close."

Cecile dropped her chin to her chest and hauled in a deep breath. Anger and frustration had carried her this far. And hope. Blustering her way through an apology only to have him refuse her left her drained and broken-hearted. A tear budded and skimmed down her cheek. "Then I guess I owe you another apology."

"And what would this one be for?"

"For making a fool of myself." She dragged a hand across her cheek, then looked up. His face was in shadows, his body only a silhouette in the darkness. She felt the moonlight on her face, cast through the cut-glass panels on either side of the front door, and wished she, too, could hide behind shadows. She felt raw, naked, totally exposed. That's what love did to a person, she thought dismally. It stripped away all your protective barriers and left you vulnerable to be crushed in the most painful way... emotionally.

And she loved him. More than she'd allowed herself to believe. And now she'd lost him.

Slowly, painfully, she levered herself from her knees to stand in front of him. To still the trembling in her fingers, she clutched her hands in tight fists at her sides. "Well, I guess I better get home." She hauled in another breath, trying hard not to cry. She rubbed her hands down her thighs, then stuck out her right one. "How about it, Coursey? Still friends?"

She held her breath, waiting for his reply. Seconds ticked by, she counted them with each thud of her heart against her breasts. Finally he reached out, but instead of taking her hand as she'd hoped, he shoved it aside.

"Not on your terms," he growled.

Cecile didn't think he could have hurt her any more, yet she fell back a step, as if he'd hit her. "What?"

"You just don't understand, do you, Cecile?" He took a step out of the shadows, and moonlight drenched his face. The eyes that met hers were dark, filled with fury and bright with unshed tears. "I love you. I think I've loved you since the day I first saw you." He caught her elbows in his hands and tugged her closer. "But I won't spend my life with a woman who doesn't trust me."

Hope surged through her. Maybe she hadn't lost, at all. "But I do trust you, Rand," she said, her words tripping over one another in her excitement to make her feelings known. "Didn't you hear me? I said I was sorry I had misjudged you. I can't tell you how awful I felt when Jack told me the truth about Amber. I—"

He shook her so hard her head wobbled on her neck like a rag doll's. "Did you hear what you just said? Yes, you forgave me, but only after Jack corroborated that Amber's merely a friend. I don't want your trust or your love if it's only offered after you've verified my facts." His fingers tightened on her elbows, digging into her skin. "Don't you see, Cecile? I want your love, but I want it unconditionally."

She stared at him, terrified by what he was asking of her. Unconditional love? She couldn't, she was no longer capable of such a commitment. "I love you, Rand," she whispered, hoping it would be enough.

"And I love you, Cecile."

She closed her eyes, drawing in a ragged breath. The words were the ones she wanted to hear, but something was missing. There was absolutely no emotion behind them. He wanted it all... or nothing. And she wasn't sure she could give it all.

"It's Denton, isn't it?" he asked. "Because of what he did to you?"

She squeezed her eyes tighter together, fighting back the memories and the flood of emotions they drew. Slowly she nodded her head. She heard as well as felt the weight of his sigh as he dragged her into his arms.

"I'm not Denton, Cecile," he murmured, his lips pressed against her hair, his hand moving to cup the back of her head. "I'd never do anything to hurt you."

The comfort was there spreading from his chest through hers, twining itself around her heart and sending a warm rush through her veins. Understanding was there, as well. She heard it in the tenderness of his voice, the gentleness of his hands in her hair and on her back. She wanted to fight it. She wanted to throw up that protective wall so he'd never see or know her weaknesses.

But he needed honesty. More, he deserved it.

She took a step back, bracing her hands against his chest to resist the temptation of the comfort she found there. Lifting her head, she opened her eyes to look deeply into his.

"You say you'd never hurt me, Rand, and I want to believe you. More than you'll ever know, I want to believe you." A shudder racked her shoulders. She lifted her chin to hold off the emotion. "But I've heard it all before. From Denton.

"Every time he cheated and got caught, he swore he'd never cheat again. That he would never hurt me again." The compassion was there, warming Rand's eyes and pulling at her. In response to it, she lifted a hand from his chest to lay it against his cheek. He covered it with his own. A smile trembled at her lips at the tenderness of the gesture. "You're a good man, Rand Coursey. I know that." She carried his hand to her breast and flattened it over her heart. "I know that here," she said, pressing her hand firmly over his. "But then my head gets involved and I get scared and—" The tears came then, tightening her throat and skimming down her cheeks. "And I react the old way. The way I did with Denton."

"Cecile—"

"No, please," she said. "Let me finish." She took a deep breath and squared her shoulders. "I want to promise you that I'll never doubt you, that you'll have my unconditional trust. But that wouldn't be honest. And you deserve more than a lie." She caught his hands in hers and squeezed for all she was worth, as if by strength alone she could will him to understand . . . and more, agree. "But I can promise you this. Every time I have doubts or questions, I'll come to you with them, and I'll listen with my heart and my head."

She held her breath while she waited, searching his face for some type of response. But for once his face was void of emotion. She hadn't a clue what was running through his mind or his heart.

"Is this a proposal?"

Cecile's eyes bugged and she sputtered a laugh. "Well, I don't know. Maybe." The smile slowly faded as the reality behind his question kicked in. "What if it is?"

Rand bent, caught her beneath the knees and brought her to his chest. "If it is, the answer is yes. But first," he said, narrowing an eye at her, "we've got to get a few things straight between us."

Cecile draped her arms around his neck, her blood racing through her veins at the contact of his body against hers. "Oh?" she asked coyly. "And just exactly what would you like to get straight between us, Doctor?"

Rand shot her a threatening look. "Besides the obvious," he said, turning for the hallway, "my name is Rand. Not Doctor, not Coursey...simply, Rand." He kicked open his bedroom door. "And I'll do the cooking." He plopped her down on his bed, then leaned over, planting a hand on either side of her. "I hate to tell you this, but you are a miserable cook."

"I'm crushed."

He frowned at the laughter he saw in her eyes. "Yeah, right." He lifted one knee to the bed, then the other, and positioned himself over her, his face bare inches from hers. "And from now on I make the rules." Cecile opened her mouth to argue the point, but quickly closed it when he narrowed his gaze at her. "If I want to romance you, I damn well will. And if I want to tell you I love you every day for the rest of our lives, I'll do that, as well. Agreed?"

She'd thought she couldn't love him any more than she already did, but her heart twisted at his words, then swelled painfully in her chest. "Yes, sir," she said, then laughed at his dour expression.

"And I want children," he said. "Lots of them, to round out our family."

The laughter slowly melted from Cecile's face. "You do?"

"Yes, I do."

"But I thought—"

He covered her mouth with his. "Cecile, please don't think. Every time you think, we get in trouble. Just feel."

Her hands came up to meet his chest. The kick of his heart against her hands drew a devilish grin. "Whatever you say, Doc—I mean, Rand." Holding him steady with her gaze, she let her palms skim down until the heels of her hands bumped the elastic of his silk, paisley shorts. Hooking her thumbs in the waistband, she stripped them to his knees, then ran teasing fingers up the inside of his thighs.

Rand groaned, throwing back his head and arching against her touch when her fingers circled him. He sighed, his breath heavy on her face as he dropped his head to lay a cheek against hers.

"Rand," she whispered at his ear, unable to resist the temptation to tease him, "I feel—"

He covered her mouth with his, his lips fever hot. "Just kiss me, Cecile. Just kiss me and never stop."

*   *   *   *   *

**Rugged and lean...and the best-looking,
sweetest-talking men to be found in the
entire Lone Star state!**

In July 1994, Silhouette is very proud to bring you
Diana Palmer's first three LONG, TALL TEXANS.
CALHOUN, JUSTIN and TYLER—the three cowboys
who started the legend. Now they're back by popular
demand in one classic volume—and they're ready to
lasso your heart! Beautifully repackaged for this
special event, this collection is sure to be a
longtime keepsake!

"Diana Palmer makes a reader want to find a Texan
of her own to love!"   —*Affaire de Coeur*

**LONG, TALL TEXANS—the first three—
reunited in this special roundup!**

**Available in July,
wherever Silhouette books are sold.**

Fifty red-blooded, white-hot, true-blue hunks
from every State in the Union!

Look for MEN MADE IN AMERICA! Written by some of
our most popular authors, these stories feature fifty of the
strongest, sexiest men, each from a different state in the
union!

Two titles available every month at your favorite retail
outlet.

In July, look for:

ROCKY ROAD by Anne Stuart (Maine)
THE LOVE THING by Dixie Browning (Maryland)

In August, look for:

PROS AND CONS by Bethany Campbell (Massachusetts)
TO TAME A WOLF by Anne McAllister (Michigan)

You won't be able to resist MEN MADE IN AMERICA!

SILHOUETTE®
Desire®

Big Bad WOLFE

WOLFE WATCHING
by Joan Hohl

Undercover cop Eric Wolfe knew *everything* about divorcée Tina Kranas, from her bra size to her bedtime—without ever having spent the night with her! The lady was a suspect, and Eric had to keep a close eye on her. But since his binoculars were getting all steamed up from watching her, Eric knew it was time to start wooing her....

WOLFE WATCHING, Book 2 of Joan Hohl's devilishly sexy Big Bad Wolfe series, is coming your way in July...only from Silhouette Desire.